The
Palmse
Music Box

The Palmse Music Box

Historical Short Stories & Humorous Tall Tales

RAE RICHEN

The Palmse Music Box
Historical Short Stories & Humorous Tall Tales

Published in the United States of America by

Back Beat Publications,
an imprint of Lloyd Court Press
3034 N.E. 32nd Avenue,
Portland, Oregon, 97212
www.lloydcourtpress.org

Cover design by Diana Kolsky
Book Design by Amit Dey

Paper ISBN: 978-1-943640-29-4
E-book ISBN: 978-1-943640-25-6

Introduction

In these tales are small miracles. Miracles can be caused by human interaction. Sometimes the cause of a miracle cannot be explained by the social or physical sciences that we presently understand.

Yet they occur. And we try to explain them.

Come along and see what you can make of these miracles.

Table of Contents

The Investment

Portland, Oregon sure isn't the Eden I remembered from when I was seven years old, and still in pigtails. Why did I never notice the rain? Drizzling. Gray sky. And way too many houses with water problems in the basement.

I flew into town last week, following leads my purchasing staff gave me. The rain hasn't let up since, but I had to come. The housing market in Portland bottomed out during the last recession. Property is a steal up here. I'm counting on the recent re-expansion of micro-chippers like Intel, and software giants like Seiki Graphics to turn property prices around. The deals I make this month will create upwards of three million dollars in the next two years. And when the money comes in, I'll be gone – where the rain can't get at me.

Most of this week, I've worked with Shirley Jensen. She's a great real estate agent, but carries a wallet full of grandchildren photos. I've decided to lure her out of Portland to work for my company – offer her a bundle and move her down to sunny Palm Springs. An attractive financial package can get almost anyone away from noisy grandchildren.

Today Shirley gave me the keys to the houses I wanted to check out. She could see I knew what to do without her. Yesterday, Shirley and I rejected six houses that were dogs. But this morning, this empty house has caught my eye. I inspected the basement and found a rusty water heater, a dead furnace, but solid, dry, concrete foundation. The careful carpentry in the original woodwork impressed me, but during the last twenty years, some clod with a hammer cut the spacious rooms into small apartments. The mess made it hard to see the original house.

Tramping out front, I turned to study the vines. Ivy scrambled up the downspout pipe, draped over every window and nearly covered the roof. Once I got the ivy under control, the roof would no doubt have to be replaced, but underneath the mess, the house was well planned and solid. With a fifty-thousand dollar down payment, plus another hundred and fifty thou in renovations, this house would make me a half a million. And the empty, and overgrown lot next door would easily bring me another hundred thousand, maybe more. Whoever left this place a shambles did me a big financial favor.

A ragged camellia, nearly obscuring the front door, looked ready to pop into bloom, but what had me suddenly squinting at the old brown shingles was the feeling that I knew this place – and should remember it. I'd never bought in Portland. Papa scorned the town. We were business partners, so until his death, I'd avoided Portland. This house can't be one of our properties.

Back in my rental car, out of the wet air, I pulled up my cell phone and punched in the number of the realty office. Got Shirley on the first try. "Shirley," I said, "This is Angela Wortham. Want to find out if there is a gas line into a residence in southeast Portland."

On her computer, Shirley can bring up lots of facts about a house. What she can't find on-line, she finds through her network of friends – the lady at the gas company, the county records – you name it, Shirley knows the contact. I could hear her tapping in the address I gave her. Within moments she came back on the phone.

"Yes indeedy, Angela. There once was a gas furnace. Service was cut off when the previous owner died, looks like twenty years ago. Nothing but rental tenants and electric baseboard heat since then.

The present owners inherited – a corporation of some sort, based in California."

"Shirley, who was the owner who died?"

I expected her to tell me it was none of my business. It wasn't either, except I wanted to clear up this feeling that I'd seen this house. To my surprise, Shirley tapped her keyboard again.

"Hmm," she said.

I stared through my drippy windshield and tensed, wishing I could see Shirley's screen. What I could see was the front gable on the house. Through the ivy I caught a glimpse of the fancy-cut on its fascia board – a three-petaled lily repeated up and down the steep face of the gable. That type of frill indicated the house was built sometime before World War I. I hadn't seen the lily design since I was a kid. Staring at it, I began to suspect the truth.

While Shirley hummed to herself, I glanced toward the empty lot and its tangle of ivy and blackberries. And then, I knew. The whole garden transformed from brambles to a hedge of Amur Maple filled with songbird nests. In my mind, stately rhododendrons, arbutus trees and rampant perennials took the place of ivy puffs and blackberry stems. In the shade, an empty settee rocked, suspended by chains from its wooden frame. Under the briars and vine whips, I knew there was an arbor constructed of fitted pipes, set in a concrete step. It had been painted dark green so as to disappear under the rose it had supported.

I opened the car door and took the phone with me as I approached the chicken wire fence. I paced ten steps from the driveway. There I found a three-by-two foot piece of broken concrete carefully laid into a patch of gravel.

Shirley came back online. "Angela?"

"Still here." I said, staring at the concrete where it disappeared – a ten-inch high step up into wild grass, ivy and a desperate straggle of woolly thyme.

"I don't find the previous owner's name," Shirley said, "but if it's important, I can make a quick call to the county records and the title company."

I straightened up, forcing myself to stop looking at that piece of my memory. I had to be pragmatic, not let the sudden tightness in my throat dictate whether I bought an asset or a liability.

"Angela?" Shirley sounded worried. "Do you need that name, Hon?"

I swallowed. "If you don't mind, I would like to know." I had to have a reason, I told myself. She'll think I've gone nuts. "I . . .I believe it might be important."

That was lame. Shirley let me hang on there for an embarrassing silence before she said, "Yah, sure. I'll get that for you."

Yah, sure. I'd never heard that phrase from her before. Suddenly, I had this image of her – a mother. A strong and tall, Scandinavian mother who would never leave her children and grandchildren.

I made sure my phone was ready to receive calls. I tried to get back to assessing the cost of renovation, and of selling off the second lot.

Then that broken concrete stair caught my eye once more, and my mind reeled back twenty-five years. I remembered wearing overalls and listening to the scruff of fabric against fabric as I walked. I closed my eyes and saw the whole day. My arms were thinner when I was seven years old – thinner and more tanned. That summer, every day, I traveled ten long city blocks to work with my Grandfather Bartolomeo Bertolucci, in Bertolucci's Flower and Vegetable Gardens.

Those ten blocks to his home helped me escape the lonely silence of my father's house. All that summer, Papa closed his office door to me. He came out only to eat meals and give orders. Especially to give orders. Everyone did what Papa ordered – the cook, the housekeeper, and me. There was a full-time gardener doing whatever Papa said – maintaining beds of annuals and stiffly staked Delphiniums, and pruning everything bald. In Papa's garden, a circular drive swooped past squared-off shrubbery; and the elm trees were never allowed to grow more than twenty-five feet tall. Only the compost behind the three-car garage was left alone to sprout weeds. Papa ordered a new compost bin built near the stump of the False Cypress, where mother's arbor and swing once stood.

Each morning, I hurried through the summer studies and piano practice Papa required, then slipped out to walk to Grandfather Bartolomeo's. Each new block I passed held smaller houses than the block before it. At the tenth intersection, I arrived at a little shopping center – a pharmacy, a Dairy Queen and a filling station. That was the corner where I turned left and ran toward his house.

I opened my eyes and stared at the mess that now covered his garden. I could still see Bartolomeo's gnarled hands and mischievous grin as he rose from his lettuce patch to greet me on that last day. I had helped him plant the lettuce in late spring and I could see it was heading up real big. The sun warmed oil from sage and rosemary shrubs, perfumed the whole garden.

Bartolomeo limped toward me, stopping under the green-pipe arbor. Trained up those pipes, around and above him, bloomed the SunBurst Yellow rose we planted together on my seventh birthday, the April day before my mother ran away from home. She and my Papa fought long and loud that night. The next day, she was gone. Gone forever.

As grandfather stood under our rose, I tried to greet him with a smile. I scuffed my tennis shoe and let out the odor of thyme between the blocks of concrete path.

"You are unhappy, my Angelina," he said. I held my mouth tight, so as not to cry. I stepped up onto the path and then, unable to be dignified, I ran at him. He opened his arms and pulled me close.

"So," he said. "It is come at last."

"I sneaked out," I whispered.

He bent over my head and said in my ear, "You must not. He has been hurt enough."

"Papa doesn't understand," I cried.

"But I do understand," he said, holding me away from him. "My little one, we can share love even if we are not in the same garden. We must celebrate the time we've had. All this summer, we have filled it with growing."

I wiped my nose on my arm. "Papa yelled at me. He says you made her leave, and now you're taking me, too."

Bartolomeo's grip on my arm tightened. "Never," he said, his voice so harsh, I glanced up quickly. His tanned face seemed lax, as if his muscles were tired. He looked down at me and spoke with careful emphasis. "I never believe she willingly left you. She loved you, and she loved your Papa."

"But she left," I said, and my eyes filled so I couldn't see his face anymore.

He handed me a handkerchief – a red bandana really. I wiped my nose on it and then pushed the back of my hand across my eyes to dry them.

"My Angel," he said, kneeling down beside me. "I will always know you love me. But it is not easy for your Papa to know you love him."

"Why, Pappy?"

He studied his ragged fingernails a moment. Then he glanced up, his brown eyes studying me from under his bristling brows. "Your Papa hopes that money will make people love him. He knows no other way. Go home. Show him how to grow vegetables."

"I will come back." I said.

But Grandfather Bartolomeo shook his head at me. "Not that way, my Angelina. You may phone me when you need to, but come here only when he will come with you."

Bartolomeo lifted me into his vegetable delivery truck and drove until we were two blocks from Papa's house. There he let me out before he started on his route. A week later, Papa moved us to San Francisco. There, we lived in one of the apartment buildings he bought.

Papa did not learn to grow vegetables. He said it was much better to own the land and rent it to the vegetable farmer. He showed me how to buy land and buildings. I learned all he had to teach me. For twenty-four years, I showed him how much I cared. I would never run away like mama.

After I became his business partner, he almost believed I loved him. But not quite.

Last November, when he lay dying, Papa said to me, "Now you will have all of my money and be happy at last."

He could not have been farther from the truth. I never had what I wanted most.

I stare at the remains of my grandfather's beauty and slump down onto the arbor step. I had left Bartolomeo, and it had not earned me my Papa.

At that moment, my cell phone rang. I fumbled it open. "Shirley?" I asked.

"Found it," she said, her voice strong and warm. "Fellow name of Bertolucci owned your house. His daughter inherited, but she was never found. It ended up going to his granddaughter's trust. The trustee has been renting it out ever since, but for some reason, put it up for sale last September."

Numb, I waited too long to answer. Shirley called into the phone. "You okay, Honey?"

I tried to sound as if my world were still whole. "I'm . . . just cold."

"Do you know the name of the granddaughter?" Shirley's voice was soft now.

"I know it, Shirl." My voice cracked with tension.

"What can I do?" she asked.

I glanced at the hidden house, and around at the remains of the garden, frantically shoring up my crumbling life. "Do you know a good garden renovator?" I asked her. "The whole place is covered in blackberries."

"You fixing up to sell?"

"No, going to buy to live." Saying it eased the pain some.

"Want to grow things?"

I took a deep breath and said, "I want to find the things that are here and bring them back to life."

"Some good old gardens, you can do that," Shirley said. "Of course you have to add some of your own choices. And there's a lot of shit to shovel."

That made me smile. "You sound like you know."

"Heck, selling houses is only a part-time fancy with me. Pays for my gardening habit. Want help?"

Through my tears, I gazed at the nearest thorn and said, "You bet I do."

Seismic Mapping

For *The Boston Blarney and News*
Dateline, Isabeau, Colorado
April 1, 1880

Hello from out west. Randall Thompsen here with a dispatch to your favorite Boston news rag.

In the spring of 1880, I have hunted up a story for you, my news readers, my dear friends back in Boston. In this pursuit, I hitched a wagon ride to the highest mining operation in the Rocky Mountains of Colorado, the site of a recent discovery – a rare seam of anthracite coal. Anthracite, like all coal, is, at bottom, merely decayed vegetable matter. Since before man walked upright, since before the large lizards stomped across the earth – those lizards whose bones are now being discovered near ancient western lake beds, since before time, this decaying matter has been subjected to the friction and heat of our moving, changing earth.

Imagine a tropical fern of twenty feet in height. It thrives at the edge of a marsh, develops hundreds of fronds, and in its lifetime, sends out millions of spores to create copies of itself. After its numbered years, in the midst of a forest of its oblivious offspring, the fern withers and dies, falling into the boggy water which once nourished its roots.

Over time, the earth moves. The bog is stirred under newly folded wrinkles in the earth's surface which we call 'mountains'. For long ages – long beyond the ability of man to imagine – the fern and its children are ground down under the enormous pressure of granite and limestone until they become dark and hard. They are anthracite coal.

Then man arrives on the earth. He discovers fire. He discovers useful tools: rock, then bronze, and then the strong metal, iron. And man discovers anthracite – a substance so hard that a sharp tool jammed into its surface and well-struck with a granite hammer flings off conchoidal chips of shining black.

Man experiments further. He finds the density of anthracite creates a fire that burns hot and long without much smoke. Wherever he finds it, man uses anthracite to help him heat metals and shape iron tools and iron weapons. With anthracite, he can create a blasting heat in his iron smelter in one half the time, and consuming one quarter of the volume of soft bituminous coal. And anthracite maintains that blistering heat more evenly than any substance man knows.

In all our vast land, the anthracite I came to see was the only seam of its kind in the United States outside of Pennsylvania – rare, and infinitely valuable. It had been a long time hiding in the ground and would no doubt be a short time – thirty-five years at most – in the hauling out. For the sake of my newspaper readers in Boston, I meant to learn all I could about high mountain coal mining before that anthracite disappeared, and before only its tailings were left to litter the earth.

In order to accomplish this task, I spent several terror-filled hours riding a jolting buckboard wagon, which the wagon master had hitched behind rump-ugly draft horses. We left the railhead town of Isabeau at sunrise, lurching ever upward, following a nearly non-existent trail of sharp turns bordered by precipitous drops. Ten hours later, bedraggled and bruised, we arrived at the mining camp among the alpine foothills of Crested Butte.

Once in the valley at the base of the butte, I rented a room above a sturdy, Swiss-built barn, heat provided by the cattle below. I also smiled and complimented my way into a place at the boarding table provided by the farmers' wife, Deirdre Freya. On my first night at Deirdre's board, I had the great luck to meet Gryffyth Williams, the Welsh-born miner who had discovered the anthracite seam which they were all there to drag out of the mountain.

Gryf was a long-faced, dark man. He was only twenty-nine years old, but his thick brows and curly hair were a salt and pepper gray; maybe his was black hair streaked with sandstone and lime flakes, or it might have been white hair strewn with coal dust. I could not, for sure, tell which.

"How did you know where to look for this coal," I asked him.

"Seismic mapping," Gryf answered, staring at his plate as if my attention embarrassed him, or as if he were trying not to look at me and laugh.

I had a feeling I was the city-bred rube, about to be taken in. Tentatively, I pursued the topic. "And what is seismic mapping?"

"You find the rock you're looking for with sound," he answered. His brevity almost convinced me that it was embarrassment that kept him from looking me in the eye. But then, across the table, his friend, Amos Jawarski set into a story that showed me the truth.

Amos hunched over, both his elbows on Deirdre's linen tablecloth. "Ain't you never heard of using sound to find something?" he asked me.

"The cat at night, maybe."

"Naw," he waved my cat idea away with his horny hand. "I mean like ya thump on a barrel and discover the whiskey's gone dry."

I nodded, now quite sure he was yanking on my idiot hat. "So, you're saying you find coal by thumping the mountain?"

"That's right, Mr. Newspaper Man." Now Amos pointed at his gawky companion. "Our Gryf here's been known to use just about anything to get a sounding out of them rocks."

Deirdre, and every man and child and at the table leaned forward, apparently eager for whatever balderdash Amos planned to give me.

"Normally," Amos drawled, "when we search for ore on the east coast, Gryf just has me hack down a big ol' pine. I kin drop one of them things so's it thunks down right next to whar Gryf sprawls on the ground. Then I counts seconds and he holds up fingers accordin' to the kind of echo he hears. You know, one finger if 'metamorphic', two if 'conglomenate' and three if the echo is that mush sound what comes out of ol' vegetation, such as coal. He's got the ears of a regular musician, our Gryf."

Next to me, a child smothered a giggle in a napkin. Amos eyed him balefully. "What's so funny, Jimmy boy?"

The child choked on laughter, "Nothin', Mr. Amos."

"Well then," Amos' face cracked a brief smile as he continued, "I tell you, pine thumping is fine fer the east, but it don't work everywhere. One year, Gryf and me was up in Montana territory, searching for gold and copper. In the high Montana mountains, the trees cain't get much bigger 'n your thumb. Don't make much thunder when you fell 'em. So, our Gryf was reduced to all kinds of lesser stratagems for soundin' the mountains, like dynamite and such.

On this one swelterin' afternoon, we was ridin' around in what he thought was prime copper territory. We heard this mighty rumble. It was gettin' closer and closer, and I started in to know that we was in the way of a herd of scared buffalo.

"Let's high-tail it." I shouted to Gryf.

" 'High-tail it?' says he, 'and give up this golden opportunity? Not on your life.'

"Right then and there he flops down off his horse, gives its rump a smack and throws himself on the ground. Wall, I'm not about to leave my buddy alone in the path of a herd like that. So, I smacks off my own glue factory and I straddles Gryf's body. I yanks off my hat and begin countin' and wavin' like you never saw.

"It must 'ov been the color of that hat – a plug-ugly mustard yaller – come from the hide of an old pack horse we once had to eat just to git ourselves out of a fix, but that there's a different story.

"Any way, I waved that ugly hat and that herd split right around us. Left us mebbe a foot of breathin' space on either side 'fore they closed in again at the far end of Gryf's big feet. I was amazed that not a one of them cows tripped on Gryf's boots, and that's a fact."

"Yup," said Amos, "Thank God them buffalo's is graceful. For twenty minutes, I stood there, wavin' my arms till they 'bout like to come off. After the first ten minutes, my throat was so full of dust and my nose so stopped up by the rancid smell of old cow hairs that I couldn't count no more.

"Finally, the last decrepit bull rumbles past us. My arms 'ov been in the air so long they are stuck up there. I can bend over, just enough to see Gryf crawling out from under a pile o' Montana dust. He wobbles to his feet and cranks my arms down before he tells me the results of his soundin'.

" 'Amos', says he, 'now that was a *thing* worth *doin*', cause not three hundred feet below us I definitely heard the *lovely* ting of copper.'

"Then, he goes and scratches some itch he's got inside his shirt and pulls out this mean lookin' snake what tooken refuge in there from the herd.

" 'Amos,' says Gryf, holdin' that spittin' critter behind the jaws, 'In honor of this beautiful big ol' snake, I believe we should call this mine The Anaconda'."

As Amos finished, there were hoots of laughter around the table. I glanced at Gryf. From under his thick eyebrows, he watched Amos, an incredulous look on his face as if he'd never heard this story before in his life.

After such a saga, my indulgent readers in Boston may laugh at me, as well, but I believe there is some buried truth in every tall tale. Remember friends, that our medieval dragons may be proved true by the existence of the giant lizards we only now unbury in Dakotas' wilderness. Who knows what truth may lurk in Amos Jawarski's yarn about thumping our western mountains in search of riches.

Yours from Out West,
Randall Thompsen

A Promise

A soulful woman lived in a lovely garden. The garden's flowers reflected bright hues of opalescent pink, sun gold, flaming red and soft, dusky purple. The leaves in the garden provided contrast to the flowers with deepest green and soul-cheering yellow. Yet, during the summer whereof I write, the woman, Janetta by name, drew little solace from the colorful array or the cooling leaves.

That year, she, who had created much of the garden, had no eye for beauty, for the most profound beauty in her life had been taken. Her sweet son, Evan, had died in his ninth year of life. And after Evan's death, Janetta's beloved husband, Robert, followed their son to the dark underworld, leaving her alone to grieve.

She no longer saw the beauty of her garden, but she did not neglect it. Once having taken on the responsibility for a life, she would not lightly put it down. Thus, she watered, fed, and pruned with care. She cleaned her pond, fed her Koi and provided them with pond lilies and swamp grasses in which to hide from the sun and a rocky shelf under which they could hide from predators.

However, her heart was not engaged in her work until one day in which a promise came to her from an unexpected source.

On that morning, Janetta absorbed sunny warmth from her deck as she watered the hanging fuchsia. A slight movement in the farthest corner of the garden caught her eye. She glanced out, across the lawn and the flower beds, into the shade cast by the large cherry tree. The darkness had moved near the back fence, in the area where just this morning she'd found several bleeding hearts smashed to the ground, as if cats had fought in the garden.

Her heart told her she'd seen the shadow of Evan, her tow-headed boy, playing in the dirt. Her head informed her that was impossible. Evan had to give up building his model village in the garden when he first became ill.

She squinted, trying to cut out the sun's brightness. Within that space, a large shadow appeared to be bent over, weeding beneath the lilac.

Robert, her heart cried. But her head told her to act reasonably. Neither Evan, nor Robert were in that darkness. Their darkness was deeper, more complete.

She leaned toward the movement. Beside the garden pond, a masked face raised up. Deep in the shade of her French lilac, the animal's solid body held rigid. His eyes wavered toward her blue watering can, perhaps assessing whether it might be a weapon. He seemed to dismiss that possibility and resumed his study of her face.

His long, faintly striped legs poised on the edge of the pond. One front paw hovered over the water. She believed he'd been about to take a drink when she surprised him. Janetta thought it a delicate gesture, that three-legged stance with one creamy paw dangling over the surface of the pool.

The raccoon's eyes held her complete attention as he moved. She knew she should be afraid for her fish. The mother-power within her struggled to break his spell, but she could not free her mind from the tug of his gaze. Slowly, the raccoon dipped his dainty paw into the water, down and down with great care and silence.

Raccoons don't move that slowly, she thought. Nevertheless, as if under a hypnotic trance, she watched as he worked with utmost deliberation.

Mesmerized, she watched his long arm reach in, right up to the armpit. He held still for endless seconds, and then rose, inching up, seeming not to break the surface tension. As the creamy fur above his wrist appeared, a thrashing form surged beneath the water. She saw a large tail whipping left then right, then left, throwing froth onto the raccoon.

His spell upon her shattered. She screamed at him. The struggling form sent waves of fear-filled water across the surface of the pond. Within his paw, she saw her gold and black spotted Koi. The fish writhed, its tail flashing, its head twisting frantically from side to side.

Vaulting the railing of her deck, Janetta yelled. She landed and ran toward the raccoon. He turned to face her, holding the fish out in front of him, as if threatening either the Koi or her. She feared he would break the Koi's back.

The raccoon lay the fish on a flagstone at the edge of the pool, turned and climbed up the lilac, bending its slender branches with his weight. He leapt onto the fence and, with a horse's stiff-legged gait, loped along the fence-cap to the neighbor's garage roof. He turned once, glanced at Janetta and then down at the gasping Koi.

Heedless of the raccoon, still dangerously close above her, she hurried to the fish, lifted its cold, slick body, and, putting no pressure on the delicate fins, she lowered it into the pool. As her hand entered the water, she opened her fingers wide enough for the round body to move away. The scales of the fish rasped across her palm as he floated out into the water.

She watched the water distort the image of her hand and the fish.

To her horror, the Koi's motionless body sank four, then five inches. With sorrow, she remembered the fullness of its belly against her fingers, and near her thumb the firm cartilage at the root of its fins. A chill raced up her back as she realized her hesitation had cost this beautiful being its life. She should have attacked the raccoon.

Then the fish flexed its gill fins. Its long tail moved with a languid stroke, stabilizing its body among the lily stems at the edge of the pond. Hope entered her heart. Her breath escaped in a prayer. The golden Koi turned its bull-nosed body. With one swish of its tail, the fish disappeared into the shadows of the pool grass.

Stunned, Janetta went limp, lowering her head to rest on the inner side of her extended arm. At that moment, within the water, she felt the brush of scales against her little finger. The feather-touch of a fin followed, then the pool once more became still.

With care, she removed her hand. Recalling the silent stealth of the raccoon, she glanced up, expecting to find him still watching from the garage – perhaps waiting until she left so he could attack the Koi.

But the raccoon was gone.

She realized what she must do, what she should have done before she ever chose the Koi for her garden. She raced inside, down into the basement, and flung open the cupboard where she kept Evan's childhood toys. Behind the Fisher-Price airport and the plastic record player, she found the wooden windmill.

Robert had made this treasure for Evan's garden village. Standing in the corner of the village where the pond now rested, it had been a whirling semblance of life and energy.

Lovingly, she lifted the mill out, wrapped her free hand about its metal armature and carried it to the garden. If her husband had been here, he would have teased her about setting the mill up as a scarecrow. But Robert had died soon after Evan, and she was left to decide what use to make of old memories.

When she emerged into the back yard, the lilac remained stiffly upright. The silent pond showed no sign of the raccoon, yet.

She cleared a place next to the pond, among the anemone for the base of the little tower and its wind sails. She set it where Evan had always put it, the place where he found a breeze on nearly any summer day – directly in line with the path down the south side of the house, where the heat of the sun set the air to moving up, and down, and around.

As surely as if Evan had been there to fuss over it, the thin, metal blades began to whirl. The motion activated a series of gears. An armature rose and fell, making the squealing sound of metal against metal that used to drive her to frequent oiling, but for which she was now thankful.

Let this noisy motion drive that raccoon far away.

After she set the windmill to work, she had time to take a breath, and the truth came to her then. The raccoon carefully had not killed the Koi. Nor had he taken the fish up the lilac tree, though the climb was so easy he certainly could have done it three legged. Instead, he had laid the fish with great care upon the rock nearest the pool, and waited atop the garage, almost urging her to come to its rescue.

She could not imagine why an animal would take such pains to capture a meal and then not keep the prize. He'd been very deliberate about every other move he made in those two minutes. She knew he didn't leave the fish because of haste or fear.

The wet print of the fish had not yet evaporated from the flagstone. As she studied the print, a motion in the pool caught her attention. A small black nose poked above the surface. The nose rose twice more as she watched.

She leaned over the water, and saw the clear golden color of the Koi, its black-spotted sides vertical within the pond. She thought it must have become very hungry after it recovered from its fright, so she reached into her apron pocket for the little box of fish food.

The incident with the raccoon had made her forget her garden routine entirely, including the ritual of feeding the Koi. She fumbled with the box lid. The Koi bobbed to the surface again, opening its mouth.

"Mommy," she heard. The food box dropped to the rock. She watched the Koi sink, wiggle its tail, and rise again.

"Mommy," it said in Evan's young voice.

Her heart skipped into her throat. She couldn't speak, afraid to awake from the spell.

"Hear me?" Evan said, on his next bob up.

Leaning toward him, she whispered, "My Evan?"

"For a time." He sank and rose to speak again. "This is work."

"What shall I do?"

"Listen. I came. You all right?"

"But that raccoon nearly . . ."

"That's Daddy. We get attention." Evan sank. Janetta glanced up at the garage, but Robert was not there.

Evan's bubbling rise made her look back at him. Yes, the same bright eyes, if a little farther apart. The same quick way about him.

"Daddy protects me."

She blinked. That was what Robert had said on the day before he took his life. *Our Evan, he is small, and without guile. He'll need someone to protect him.*

Evan flipped to his belly and swam amongst the lily stems. Her heart cringed to see him disappear. She reached out, putting her hand carefully into the water, hoping for his fin to brush her again. Waiting, she wondered at her sanity, her willing belief that this fish was her son returned a year after his death.

Glancing at the broken bleeding hearts, she saw that their crushed stems and branches had hidden a large area of scuffled earth. Beyond, several iris and a portion of the Daphne bush lay smashed against the fence. She began to guess the meaning of the mess.

A soft fin brushed against her thumb. And then Evan rose, using her forearm to help keep himself upright.

"You see? Daddy fought tomcat?"

"I . . . Was Dad hurt?"

"Yes. He will die. And that's why we must leave."

"Oh, please . . ."

"Don't be sad. We're assigned to be brothers in the next life."

She bit her lip to hold back her protest.

"Isn't that funny?" he asked.

Nothing was funny. She wished to beg them to stay, but she'd seen that life as a fish was precarious. It would be cruel to ask him. "Brothers with Robert? Yes, that's . . . that's a good one."

"If you wait, Mother, we can . . ." Evan had tired. He sank again to swim in the refreshing water.

She wanted desperately to know what he meant by "wait", but even more desperately, she wanted him to regain his strength. She remembered how the medicine had tired him during those months. Never again could she watch him grow pale and dark-eyed as he had then.

Moments passed. Her hand went numb with cold, but she would not remove it from the pond. Beside her, the windmill creaked and whirled. The leaves of the lilac rustled in the breeze, but when she glanced up to the garage roof, Robert was not there.

At last, she felt the fin, and the swish of Evan's tail as he rose.

"Wait. Live long." he bubbled.

"Yes," she said. He looked so worn from standing on his tail that she promised without asking why. And then he rose higher, on a powerful stroke.

"Brothers while you live good life," he said. "Then we again with you. They promised."

With a flash of gold and a brush of tail, he vanished into the grasses and lilies.

Janetta lay by the pool that night. Sometime after the moon rose, the windmill stopped turning. When the raccoon came, she saw by the moonlight that a deep cut crossed his belly. He moved stiffly when he reached out and flipped the windmill armature just enough to loosen it – a gesture Robert had used often.

The sails moved again in the breeze. Watching her, the raccoon lifted the fish from the pool and held the Koi gently to his chest. He faced her fully. The fish did not fight him.

She raised her hand. In the moonlight she saw his mask tilt toward her before he hugged the calm Koi to his heart, climbed up the lilac and disappeared.

How To Build A Wooden Boat

Estonia,
The Year 1978

At the kitchen garden of the old manor, the big housekeeper grabbed the face of five-year-old Anja, her daughter. She yanked Anja's straight black hair. Anja pulled from her mother's grasp and kicked her mother in the shins.

Ten-year-old Mikhel Aivar Krichevsky stared at them through the open door of the woodshop. This was not the first time he had seen Anja fight back when her mother beat on her.

"Mikhel. Focus!" Mr. Jarve Saarela said.

In the woodshop at Palmse Manor, Estonia, Mikhel tried again to pay attention to Jarve Saarela, as the old man showed him how to bend the thin boards, but the scene outside worried him.

Mikhel's friend, Velo held one end of the board, ready to dip the length into the mixture in the vat, the mixture Jarve said would open up the wood fibers and let the board become a new shape.

But Mikhel held his end poised in the air. He couldn't stop watching the scene near the manor house kitchen. The housekeeper slapped Anja and screamed at her in Estonian.

Mikhel shrank inside, wincing with every blow. He tried to think how to save the little girl. He didn't understand why the woman screamed in Estonian when most of the time she pretended she understood only Russian.

A moment later, Jarve Saarela spoke in a low growl. "Lad, you can do nothing. I am her uncle, and I cannot stop her mother."

"But Anja," Mikhel said.

Velo finally spoke. "One day she will pop her mother and be done with her."

"I will pop her mother first," Mikhel said.

Jarve said, "Better you should be Anja's friend. Show her how a calm heart talks to others."

Mikhel remembered all the times that Jarve took his little niece on a hike or let her play and help in his wood shop. Jarve did as he wanted Mikhel to do.

"Yes, Mr. Jarve," Mikhel said.

"And now, let the kerfed wood down into the vat where we can soak it and bend it."

Mikhel and Velo knew the vat was filled with a mixture of horse urine and water, but Jarve had somehow taken all piss smell out of it. Besides, he explained that urine was sterile. It was manure that needed to have impurities killed with heat and time.

Mikhel loved the smell of the wood, loved learning how to kerf it so that it could bend, a skill his grandmother said she also used in sewing his shirts. She showed him how she cut into the seam just enough so that the neck and arm holes bent and fit with ease.

Velo asked, "Why do we want a shaped vegetable bed?"

Jarve glanced around, as if making certain no one heard him. "We learn these skills because I want you to know how to create a shape, and because I want you boys to know how to make a water-tight box."

"Won't the lining material make it water-tight? Mikhel asked, his eyes still straying to the girl. Her mother punched her in the stomach.

Mikhel jerked back from the vat.

Jarve said. "Don't react. Don't look."

Anja sat hard in the dirt of the path. Her mother stomped into the back door of the manor house.

"Let Anja keep her pride," Jarve said. "Later, go to her and ask her to play with you. Kindness will become her strength."

Mikhel nodded as if he could stop worrying and do as Jarve said..

Velo insisted. "What good is a water-tight box?"

Jarve didn't answer. He stood and glanced out the back window of his woodworking shop, in the opposite direction from the manor house.

Mikhel followed his gaze. There, beyond a few heathers, birch and pine trees, lay the dilapidated boat house on the shore of Palmse Lake. Mikhel knew the lake as a wide spot in a little creek that probably fed the Loobu Jogi. The Loobu then ran into the Ohepald wetland.

The wetland, he'd heard, emptied into the Baltic Sea, but he had never been allowed near the sea. Beyond the sea lay Finland, Denmark, Germany, the world of treacherous capitalists, the world his teachers scorned.

*　*

However, Mikhel knew the boundaries of what once had been his grandfather's farm before the Soviets removed his grandfather to the east, to Siberia. Mikhel walked those lands frequently, thinking about the man taken from his land in the dark days after the war. Ten-year-old Mikhel had never met him, being born well after those times, but he could follow the work of that man in the un-tilled hillocks and the ponds of his small holding. The old farm sat at the neglected edges of the collective. His grandfather's voice seemed to rise from the birch trees.

My Mikhel, Grandfather whispered, *rescue our land. Raise our people.*

But Mikhel could see that was not possible. He couldn't even take care of little Anja, who was ruled by her powerful and angry mother.

The collective farm surrounding Palmse Manor grew unhappy rye and barley, thin rice in the boggy areas, sugar beets, potatoes, and, everywhere, tomatoes and cucumbers in greenhouses. Dairy goats and milk cows scoured the fields for edibles.

The pines of the forest struggled in the rocky lowland of northern Estonia. At latitude fifty-nine, winter's darkness was long, summer sunshine short. Drink seemed to be the best friend of many.

As he grew older, Mikhel saw that drink and envy drove the mother of Anja.

Mikhel understood the attraction of drink. Anja's father had been taken to Siberia before she was born – that same kind of sweeping away of the men of Estonia that had happened sometimes at the whim of the Russians.

Drink clouded sorrow. Drink made people laugh and shortened the long dark nights.

But his grandmother and his mother had not taken to alcohol when grandfather disappeared. Mikhel and his mother and father lived with Grandma in her small cottage at the edge of the old farm. His father helped grandma grow vegetables in the garden surrounding her home. Together, they raised chickens, five ewes and one ram.

Each year, Grandma picked one ewe for slaughter. The meat flavored her soups for half of the year. The fleece of the other ewes gave her yarn. Spinning, knitting and gardening brought Grandmother money. Many in the nearby shops ordered and waited for her wool sweaters. A friend sold Grandmother's sweaters in the market of the city, Tallinn.

And each year, the ewes dropped new sheep that could be kept or sold as needed.

Elsbeth Krichevsky, Mikhel's mother, cooked for the cooperative managers who lived in the old German manor house. Mother's cooking also kept the family fed.

One day, having a snack in the kitchen, Mikhel asked his mother. "Why did you marry Papa?"

His mother laughed. "You wonder because he is Russian and a guard?"

"Well, yes."

"Ivar Krichevsky loves to sing and read. And, in order to court me, he learned to speak Estonian."

Later, Mikhel asked Papa Ivar, "Why did you marry Mama?"

"I heard her singing in the kitchen. She taught me Estonian through song, and she taught me to care for others."

Ivar spoke Estonian to Mikhel at home and Russian when they were near the overseers and the managers of the collective farms. He learned to sing the old songs of Estonia and taught Elsbeth and Mikhel the songs of his Russian childhood.

Mikhel's friend, Velo, loved to come to Grandmother's. Most of the year, Velo lived in an apartment building constructed by the Soviets.

"Gray. Everything is gray in the town," Velo said. "Walls, streets, even the graffiti fades to gray after a winter on the concrete walls. I like the colors of your grandmother's home."

When they had turned ten years old, Mikhel and Velo had gone to work after school at the manor house with Jarve Saarela, who, besides teaching them how to make water-tight boxes and shaped wooden structures, was the handy-man for repairs to the many buildings and the barns of Palmse Manor House.

During one of the many times that Estonia was ruled by Germany, the Palmse Manor had belonged to the Von der Pahlen family. During Estonia's freedom years between the world wars, there were accommodations made for the family. But basically, Estonians ran the land. However, ever since the second world war, the Von der Pahlens were a memory. After the war, the Soviets had collectivized the farms, exported Estonian intellectuals and politicians and placed commune managers in the quickly deteriorating manor house.

So, by 1978, when he was eleven, Mikhel had only known the manor house as the home of the manager of the communal farm. Inside the manor house, where his mother worked, there lived for several years, the newest farm manager's family, the Ligachevs. Mr. and Mrs. Ligachev had a son, Sergey, who at eighteen was far older than Mikhel. Sergey walked around the house and farm with his back stiff and his short brown hair always combed. He never talked to anyone who worked on the collective or in the manor.

Mikhel began to realize that collective and communal life in the Soviet Republic of Estonia distributed itself unevenly. Some had more. Many, less.

More seemed to be the lot of the cooperative managers, those who were sent from Moscow or Tallinn to run everything. More came also to those who spoke Russian all the time and neglected to teach their children to understand Estonian.

*   *

One morning eating left-over breakfast in the manor house kitchen, Mikhel asked his mother, "Why does the manor house have more food than the cooperative farmers?"

"Shh," she hissed, looking around her. "Not to be discussed here."

"But the manager sends most of the food raised here away to Tallinn or Leningrad. The farmers have very little."

The kitchen door swung open. In marched Anja's mother, pulling seven-year-old Anja by the ear, hissing, "You do not tell me how to do my job, Missy."

She stopped and stared at Mikhel's mother.

"Did I hear you speaking Estonian?"

"To my son, yes."

She let go of Anja's ear and said, "You know the Ligachevs don't understand Estonian. How are they to know you are not planning sedition?"

"First,"Mother said,"The Ligachevs understand more than they let on, and second, they would see that I'm talking to a twelve-year-old."

Mikhel said, "What is sedition?"

"I'm not talking to you, Boy."

Mother said, "His name is Mikhel, and he asked you a civil question which you now may answer."

Anja's mother glared at Mikhel, but to his surprise she said, "Uhmm, sedition is planning against the Soviet way of life."

Mikhel said, "Why would anybody do that?"

"Because … because seditionists are sly and slippery no-goods."

"Mikhel," mother said. "Take Anja with you to school."

He was glad to escape.

As he and Anja went out the door, he heard his mother talking to Anja's mother. "If you want to be Russian, then be Russian, but don't abuse your daughter just because Mrs. Ligachev abuses Sergey."

Mikhel looked at Anja, hoping she had not heard or understood. But Anja stared back into the kitchen. Mikhel slammed the door and took her hand for the walk to their one-room school.

*   *

Inside the musty old school, Anja sat with other seven-year-olds on the woodstove side of the room. Mikhel watched her from his colder side with the older children. She seemed to be seething inside, and he worried what might happen. He was certain it would happen, but he hoped to stop it early.

So, he wasn't paying attention when the teacher pulled down the map of the Soviet republics and asked the students to name them all. The list began in the singsong voice of group recital by the bored.

"Estonia, Latvia, Lithuania, Czechoslovakia, Hungary, Yugoslavia, Ukraine, Afghanistan, Kazakhstan, …

"Not true yet," Anja shouted from her side.

Mrs. Blumen stared at her and then said, "What are you shouting about?"

But Mikhel knew she had been listening to Uncle Jarve.

Anja insisted. "The Soviets don't own Afghanistan yet. And they won't, if the people there keep their freedom."

"Young lady, you are being rude."

Mikhel stood up, nearly knocking Velo off their bench. "Mrs. Blumen, why does Russia want Afghanistan? What do they have? Gold or oil?"

"You will sit down, Mr. Krichevsky. You know better than to interrupt our recitation."

Velo pulled on his shirt tail. "Sit. Sit." Velo whispered.

On the other side of the room, Anja sat with her head bowed over her papers. Her seat partners leaned away from her. It appeared Mrs. Blumen had forgotten the beginning of the interruption.

But at noon, Mrs. Blumen kept both of them in from lunch and recess, a silent time-out on separate sides of the room.

After school, Anja said, "Don't ever do that again."

"Do what?"

"Don't distract the teacher from my questions. I'm not your little sister, so let me get in trouble without you."

"Stop calling her out about mistakes."

"Do you want her to teach lies to the whole school?"

Mikhel wished she didn't listen to her Uncle Jarve. She learned too much.

*   *

Doing repairs with Jarve in the old manor house, Mikhel found remnants of a time when color seemed to be a huge part of life:

painted walls, wallpaper, now faded, but elegantly patterned, fabric on furniture that still shown in the buried seams with what once had been the most beautiful reds and yellows. Though now grayed, the colors were almost as beautiful as Grandmother's home-dyed yarns.

In the back hall at Palmse Manor, there stood a box of about three and a half feet in height. It had sturdy, slightly curved legs. Its wooden sides had been painted black, or, as Mikhel believed, it's mahogany stain had gone black over many years.

On one side of the box hung two cymbals and a small drum head. No armature protruded from the nearby slits in the box, but Mikhel figured something used to come out. From the wear on the drum head and the shine on part of the cymbals, he knew that at one time, the bells and the drum played, but they had been silent all the years of his life.

Once, he got down on his knees to look inside, assuming that the mechanism was in the box.

At the moment, he had his hand on the latch for its back door, his father came behind him, grabbed his arm and said, "Never touch that. Ligachev, will be extremely angry if you do."

His father, usually so calm and friendly, had such fear in his eyes that Mikhel determined never again to touch the thing. He walked around it and made certain never to even brush against its aged wood corners.

*   *

The music box was a curiosity, but to Mikhel, the most important part of the house stood in the west parlor, a grand piano. Not to be touched, but shining cherry wood in the case, and inside, golden and silver strings in a harp-like shape on top of the spruce sound board.

Mikhel worked in that room as much as he was allowed, polishing the furniture, cleaning tobacco stains and coffee from the upholstery or the carpet. Mikhel, now twelve-years-old, hovered, and watched Sergey, the son of the manager, practice the piano.

One morning, Mikhel entered the house to help Jarve find the source of a water leak in the parlor. As they came inside the back door, Mikhel heard someone playing the piano. This was not the manager's son. This was someone who plucked tentatively, trying to find a tune, which Mikhel recognized as one of the children's songs his mother sang when he was a baby – a song she often sang while she cooked in the manor kitchen. The one plucking also sang the song in the high, clear voice of a child.

Mikhel opened the door to the piano room. At that moment, the manager's son burst past him. He shouted in Russian and hit seven-year-old Anja Saarela on her ear.

Mikhel howled and tackled the boy by the knees. Sergey was much bigger, and six years older than Mikhel. He scrambled out from under Mikhel's skinny body and grabbed Mikhel by the arms.

Anja danced around the two of them crying and reaching in to hold the arms of the bigger boy. She failed to stop him as he landed a punch to Mikhel's jaw and another to his stomach.

"That's enough, Sergey." The voice was Jarve's. "Enough," Jarve lifted the bigger boy and set him on the worn carpet. "Anja has learned not to touch the piano and Mikhel has learned not to tackle boys who are older. What have you learned?"

Sergey glared at Jarve. "I will tell my father about this. You will not be working here any longer."

"That will work out quite well for me. Your father can do all the repairs and build all the buildings. I will work in some more pleasant place."

Sergey backed up.

"What have you learned, Sergey?"

"Not to leave the door to the piano parlor unlocked."

"That is one possible lesson. Another?"

The boy's eyes darted to the hallway. "Not to trust you."

"Fair enough. Then it is mutual."

Sergey's glance came back to Jarve's face. "I will tell."

"Please do so."

Jarve ushered both Anja and the bleeding Mikhel out of the house. "We will leave the leak for a few days and let Sergey, or his father, think about what has happened."

They stepped into the kitchen near the back door. Mikhel's mother cleaned the blood from his nose and put ice on Anja's face where the print of an open palm left a red mark.

"Where is Anja's mother?" Jarve asked.

"Counting bottles in the wine cellar," Mikhel's mother answered.

Jarve glanced at Anja and merely hovered over her.

Mikhel's nose and Anja's cheek both sported cloths filled with ice.

Anja said. "It is not fair that Sergey gets to play the piano. I want to play the piano, and it just sits there for twenty-three and a half hours a day."

Mikhel looked at her quickly, saw that in the last few months she had grown. At seven, she had long legs and clear ideas of justice. She neared his own height.

He wondered how long it would be before she did as Velo had predicted and popped her mother, or tried to pop Sergey.

"Anja," he said. "You have a nice voice, and that voice doesn't belong to Sergey. So, you can sing."

"Mother won't allow me to sing in the manor house because I always sing in Eesti."

Mikhel's mother checked Anja's bruised face. "Don't you know some songs in Russian?"

"I hate Russian. Eesti songs are more pretty.

Jarve spoke to Mikhel's mother. "Elsbeth, is Ivar still guarding at Illumagi Chapel?"

"He is."

"I believe he can help with this situation. I will go see him now while the children recover. May I leave them with you?"

"We'll be fine. We will make some kuchen."

Mikhel and Anja grinned at each other. It seemed they could already smell sugar and butter.

Mikhel's mother began humming a tune and pulling out sugar and flour for kuchen. Mikhel chimed in with a harmony to her humming. After a few moments of listening, even Anja made up her own alto part to the song. When they finished. Anja said, "What is that song?"

Elsbeth spoke in Russian. "Oh honey, that's *In the Meadow Stands a Birch Tree.*"

"Oh," Anja said. "Well, maybe some Russian songs are pretty."

"Yes, and many Russian people. It is not Russians that keep us down. It is the Soviet method of controlling others."

Moments later, Anja said, "Let's sing it again."

Mikhel began it again, this time with Russian words. After two verses, Anja joined him in Russian with a new high obligato.

*   *

Two days later, Papa Ivar drove Anja, Velo and Mikhel on an excursion up a nearby hill. The woods around them smelled of new needles and bark. The last sign before they rounded a corner, said 'to Illumagi Chapel'. When the road turned, they saw an ancient cemetery and a whitewashed building with a long, sloped roof. The small building looked to be about one and a half stories tall. Its front section stood twenty feet taller than the rest and wore a steep-sided hat on its small tower. They had never been inside of this little building. Papa Ivar explained that it once had been a place for people to worship.

"Worship?" Velo said, "What's that?"

Mikhel said, "That's talking to God." He knew about praying because his mother still prayed secretly when they were at home, and she taught Mikhel some memorized prayers.

Velo looked around at the stored guns and ammunition, the barbed wire rolls and unexplainable electric wires. "This place smells like cardboard and oil. Why talk to anybody in here?"

"Look at that window," Anja said. The window lay partly hidden by stored material. The small section that could be seen had colored glass shining with sunlight.

"What's that for?" Velo asked.

Ivar didn't answer any of their questions. He just kept walking through the boxes and racks of rifles. He came to a set of steps and said, "You good at climbing stairs?"

"I'm good at running up the stairs," Anja said, and started to show them, her long legs moving fast.

Velo and Mikhel smiled at each other. Mikhel thought, *No wonder she's in trouble all the time. She does before she thinks.*

But he followed her, more dignified, and ready to catch her if she stumbled.

Ivar followed all of them. "Stop at the attic level and wait for us," he said.

Arriving at the upper level, Mikhel and Velo found Anja exploring nearby rooms.

"Papa said to wait," Mikhel said.

"I'm waiting," she said.

"If there are dangerous guns on the main floor, you don't know what might be up here," Velo said.

"I don't see anything but wooden boxes. What's this word?" She pointed at the side of one box.

Mikhel said, "It is Russian for explosives."

Ivar arrived. "Anja, wait means wait, not poke around. I can't bring you places if I cannot count on you to stop when I tell you to stop."

She stared at him. "But I'm waiting."

"If I told you to stop at the top of the stairs, would you still be poking into the rooms?"

"I want to know …"

"So, the answer is yes. You would not do as told."

Anja looked at her shoes. She glanced at Mikhel, who waited. She glanced at Velo who studied his fingernails.

"I'm sorry, Mr. Ivar. I won't poke next time."

"All right. I will remind you." He turned left and opened the first room. "See what is in here?"

All three of them looked into the room, and all three stared in silence. At last, Anja spoke. "A piano!"

*   *

That was the day they began piano lessons. It didn't matter that the rest of the building was full of explosives, this room was theirs. Ivar made a lock for it. They cleaned it of cobwebs and mice droppings. They polished the piano and found a bench they could use. All three of them took lessons at first from Mikhel's papa, who taught them how to tune the strings, and how to avoid the missing strings as they played simple chords.

Jarve came to install new strings, ordered from Tallinn as they could afford them. The piano became the best thing in their lives.

Later, as they learned more and more complicated pieces, a woman named Jannsen came to the chapel once a week to give them lessons and understanding of music theory.

Velo said, "The chapel is white. The insides are brown and gray and dirty, but the piano is all the colors."

Anja said, "That's nice, Velo. I will use it in my next poem."

"You don't write poetry," Mikhel said.

She stomped her foot. "I don't show it to you."

Velo laughed, but Mikhel just stared. He thought he knew Anja, but here was a secret one he didn't know at all."

It was Mrs. Jannsen who suggested, "We must begin also a children's choir, because they love to sing, and their voices are strong."

So, they traveled once a week to her home near Viitna Lake. Her home was next to a ski rental cabin, but she was the manager of the rental. On weekdays when the skiers returned to Tallinn, the choir practiced in the cabin's large salon.

At first, they were joined only by the children of Viitna, but later, children from other farms and settlements nearby joined them until they had thirty choir members.

Since the parents also drove the miles from their farms, Mrs. Jannsen asked Ivar, Mikhel's father, to work with them and begin an adult choir. Some grumbled that Ivar was a Russian, and in the military, but since he knew so many Estonian songs, and spoke to everyone in Estonian, the grumbling died away. The farm families loved the cooking and the sweet singing voice of Mikhel's mother, so all went well.

*   *

In between the piano lessons and the evenings of singing, Velo and Mikhel still worked with Mr. Jarve in the woodshop. Since the event in the manor house piano room, Jarve had Anja join them. She wasn't big enough to handle some heavy tasks, but she could soon bend wood into a jig and drive a nail.

After they built the shaped garden boxes, Mr. Jarve asked them to create caulk for the boxes. They began by learning to put cotton in between the boards and the framing material. They created small boxes for practice.

Next, Jarve wanted them to make caulk by getting sap from the trees.

"Why not let them leak?" Mikhel asked. "Won't the plants get water-logged and die if the boxes cannot let out water?"

"We are going to learn how to get by with less water by conserving it," Jarve said. "First, I want you to understand the sap of the three major types of trees in our woods. What are they?"

Mikhel looked outside at the hillsides. "We have a lot of birch, and some pine."

"And some cottonwood by the river," Anja said.

"Right," Jarve said. "But you won't be going into the woods near the sea."

Velo told Anja why. "The soviets put explosive mines in the whole area. Anywhere near the sea is off limits."

Anja asked, "Is that why there are so many rotting fishing dories around the commune farm?"

Jarve nodded. "They have not been allowed in the sea since 1943."

"But today, let's do a test." Jarve pointed to three cans filled with a sticky material. "Here is some pine pitch, some cottonwood pitch, and here is birch pitch. I've mixed them with ash so that they are easier to work with."

He showed them how to melt the pitch over a heated can full of water, "Like a double boiler in the kitchen" Jarve said.

Then, with a small stick, they picked up some of the pitch and applied each type to the cotton-filling inside of the small copies of their garden boxes.

Two days later, the pitch had dried, so they took the small boxes to the lake and set them afloat. Not too long into the afternoon, the box of cottonwood pitch had sunk into the lake. A day or so later, the birch box sank, but the pine caulked box kept bobbing about in the breezes and the currents of the lake.

Later in the week, Velo came to Mikhel and said," These garden boxes are a lot more complicated than necessary. We could just line them with thick plastic if we want them to be waterproof, and I still don't get why we'd want water-proof boxes anyway."

Mikhel shook his head. "I don't get it either, but Mr. Jarve always has something in his mind. Let's wait and see where he's going."

*   *

One afternoon, at Viitna, the children took a break from choir practice. Mikhel and Velo played soccer with other boys, when suddenly, they noticed a fight among the girls.

Mikhel's felt his skin tighten. He knew the fight surrounded Anja.

"Stay away," Velo said.

But Mikhel already stormed into the middle of the girls. "Leave her alone!" he shouted.

Anja turned her bloodied face and screamed at him, "Leave me alone."

Then she whacked one of the bigger girls in the stomach. That girl sat hard on her pants. Some waded into the fight pushing Anja to the ground again. Others turned on Mikhel.

"Get out of this," one girl yelled at him. "Not your fight."

At that moment, someone smacked him on the back of his head. As he went down, he heard Mrs. Jannsen. "That's enough, boys and girls. We do not fight at my house."

He saw his father lift Anja from the ground, and her kicking and yelling, "He is not a spy. He is not a spy."

*   *

Inside the Jannsen parlor with the parents and the children, Mrs. Jannsen said, "Our choir is one. One people working together. We don't accuse each other of spying, and we don't play those games that make us hate one or make another feel less important. Any who cannot live with this rule is not a member of the choir."

"But ..." Anja started.

"No argument and no 'buts'. Do you understand?"

"But..." she said again.

"Anja Saarela, you will not sing tonight. Sit in the hall until we are finished with practice."

Mikhel started to stand, but Velo pulled him down, whispering. "She won't learn to stay out of fights if you always take her side."

Mikhel started to whisper "But" until Velo shut his mouth with a stick of pine-pitch gum.

Anja sat in the hallway between the adults and the children's choirs for an hour and a half. When they finished rehearsal, Anja showed Jarve something she had written during exile.

"Well," Jarve said, "Our newest Lydia Koidula."

"Who?" Anja asked.

"Our famous poetess."

She stood straighter and walked to the truck ahead of them all.

Mikhel wished she wanted to show him. He didn't understand this angry and secretive Anja. And he was five years older than the little twerp.

*   *

Later at home, Mikhel overheard his father talking to his mother.

"One of the girls said that Mikhel was a spy because he was my son, and therefore half Russian."

"Anja needs to learn what is worth fighting for and what can be laughed at."

"Yes, but so does Mikhel," Papa said. "Wading in as he did only provided more fuel to the accusation. He just assumed that Anja needed help."

"Hmmph," his mother said. "That girl can start wars. Let her also finish them."

Mikhel frowned. She fought to protect his reputation. She had a bloody nose by the time he got there. Why did his mother think he shouldn't have helped?

*   *

Jarve had them on the floor of the woodshop. A section of the floor, about four meters by four meters, had been painted white.

"Aha!" Anja said, "So, wood shavings can be swept. Who would have guessed?"

Jarve just chuckled and handed her a piece of paper with his small handwriting on it. For the next hours, Anja read from the list of dimensions Jarve gave her. Mikhel wore his knees out on the white floor, drawing and measuring. Velo pulled a string taut from one point to another and made a mark.

Two hours later, they could see that they were drawing a pattern for the case of a grand piano.

"Mr. Jarve," Mikhel said, "We can't build a piano. We have no sound board, and not enough scrap wood even to begin on the case."

"Maybe not now, but someday we may have enough, and now, you have learned how to make a pattern. "Let's make a jig for each curve."

Velo glanced at Mikhel and frowned. They had been worried for a year or so. Mr. Jarve seemed to be teaching them to do things that did not need to be done or could not be done. How old was Jarve?

"Velo," Jarve said. "You are charged with storing these lists of dimensions in the room you share at the home of Mikhel's grandmother. No one else should see them."

"Yes, Mr. Jarve."

"Anja, you cannot mention these measurements because if you do so, we will never be able to work together again."

"Yes, Uncle."

"Next week a storage sled that breaks through snow."

"Velo and Anja can draw that one," Mikhel said. "My knees are tired. I'll read the dimension list."

*   *

In 1983, Velo and Mikhel were already fifteen years old. On a fall morning in that year, Mikhel's mother said, "Listen."

Papa Ivar turned up the radio on the kitchen counter. Grandma, Velo and the whole family leaned to hear better. The voice in Russian spoke vigorously.

"Our air force has shot down an incursion into Soviet air space. The United States and South Korea pretend this was a passenger jet from South Korea, but the U.S. air force has been threatening our air space since last spring. The Soviet Socialist Republics will not allow these incursions, and these lies to stand without confrontation."

Mikhel's mother looked at Ivar. "Our army is still in Afghanistan," she said. "Now this. When will we learn not to start wars we cannot finish?"

"Elsbeth," Ivar said glancing at Velo and his son, "They are only fifteen. We will be through with all this soon."

"Papa," Mikhel said. "Where is this news coming from? It has no static."

Ivar barely glanced at him. "It comes from our new tower near Tallinn."

"I thought that radio-TV tower was for the Olympics."

Ivar seemed startled, "Tallest thing for miles around…You didn't think they were going to such trouble just for the games, did you?"

"No," Mikhel's mother hissed. "They will use it to tell us whatever they want us to believe, and much louder, forever."

Ivar put a hand on her arm. "Careful, my Elsbeth."

Velo said, "We need an Estonian radio station."

Grandma said, "You dream, Velo."

*   *

Mikhel had the job of cleaning out the horse stalls when he wasn't working with Uncle Jarve. One afternoon, Sergey brought his mare,

Thunder, into the barn. He stumbled toward the stall and began to lift off his saddle.

Mikhel said, "Let me hang the saddle for you."

But Sergey just stared at him. "Why would you do something that is not required?"

Mikhel stepped back, surprised. "I offered because you and Thunder both look very tired."

"Because we look tired . . ." Sergey whispered.

Mikhel couldn't tell if the whisper was sarcasm or misunderstanding. He said, "I would make the same offer to my father, or anyone else who looked as tired as you look today."

Sergey stood very still, facing his mare. Finally, he said, "I have been told that you hate me."

Mikhel shook his head. "I don't know you. How could I hate you?"

"Just because I'm the one with the horse – would that not be enough reason?"

"I like Thunder, and you ride her very smoothly. I could not do that."

Sergey shifted the saddle in his arms and said, "I wish to be cavalry, but there is no such thing anymore, so I have to ride now, before I leave for the war in Afghanistan."

Mikhel smiled. "Cavalry? With a sword and a mustache?"

Sergey laughed. "A very long and dashing mustache."

"Thunder would shy away from such a mustache."

Sergey leaned against Thunder and said, "She is smarter than most of the ladies I know."

"Here," Mikhel said, taking the saddle. "I know where this goes and how to rub it down. How about if you rub down your lady love there."

Sergey stared at him and then guffawed. "You just made a very naughty suggestion, my friend."

Mikhel thought back to what he had said. "Oh . . ." he said. "Well, you are old enough and she is old enough, so I guess it's all right."

"My God!" Sergey said. "You are great! But don't say stuff like that in front of my father. He believes I don't know about any of what the Brits call hanky-panky. He hears you and he'll be sure you taught me, you sly Estonian, you."

Mikhel laughed. "Yes, I'm so sly I didn't think about what I said until you laughed at me."

"Well, at fifteen, why would you think that way?" Sergey stopped. "Or do you . . . think that way?"

"No idea what you're talking about," Mikhel said, pretending more sophistication than he really had.

He found himself suddenly wishing he really did know more about that kind of stuff – more about hanky-panky and girls. He didn't understand most of the girls he met in choir or school."

"Well," Sergey said, "Let me tell you that I plan to know more when I go away to college in Tallin next year."

"Next year? Already?"

"My mother won't let me enlist, so college is the next best way to escape her."

Mikhel didn't say anything. Mikhel knew if he agreed to the need to escape, that Sergey would feel the need to defend her. He also knew that Sergey really should get away from the mother who taught Sergey that he was hated by everyone around him.

So, Mikhel merely said, "What will you study in college?"

"I shall study how to change the world and how to attract the ladies."

Mikhel laughed, took the brush from Sergey, and continued rubbing down Thunder. "I think changing the world might be easier."

Sergey raised his eyebrows, sat on a bale of straw and said, "Man, I believe you."

*   *

One evening a few weeks later, Mikhel heard angry voices in the salon and then heard the unmistakable voice of Anja.

"You won't," Anja screamed. "You will not."

He pushed on the door of the salon and saw ten-year-old Anja held over the back of a chair by one of the Russian servants. The arm of Sergey's mother, Mrs. Ligachev, flung back, her riding crop in her hand, ready to strike Anja.

Mikhel stepped back, meaning to get help when he ran into the black box. Its cymbals rang, its drum thumped. He even heard a few notes from the broken cylinder inside.

The yells in the salon stopped. He had distracted the wife of the manager from her purpose, so he rang the bells again and hit the drum. Inside, a few more plinky notes clinked out a partial tune.

Bootsteps thumped toward him. Small feet ran out of the salon and down the hall behind him. Hoping to keep their attention off of Anja's escape, Mikhel cranked the armature that once ran the Palmse Music Box. Grinding and scraping seemed to drop the cylinder inside to the floor of the box.

The Ligacheva's riding crop split his head and racked his back, over and over.

*   *

Mikhel might have heard about the uproar in the village and in the manor house, but since he was unconscious for many days, he wasn't aware of what happened.

As the light of the gray afternoon crept across his hospital bedspread, Mikhel heard the door creak open. He couldn't move his head to see who came in. He hoped it was his father, or maybe someone with pain pills.

Anja tiptoed into his line of sight, her gaze checking his bandages and his wakefulness.

"Ah," he said. "You are all right."

"Mr. Ligachev took her riding crop and forbade her anymore beatings."

"That is good."

"But your mother refused to cook for them anymore."

That news startled Mikhel. "How will mother feed us all if she is not cook?"

"Ligacheva thought she would get my mother to cook. Within three days, my mother was just the housekeeper again."

"Doesn't Mrs. Ligachev know how to cook?"

Anja shook her head. "Neither does my mother. So far, she's tried three cooks from the village, but the villagers put in too much salt, or bad cheese or sage."

Mikhel frowned. Thoughts hurt his head. He closed his eyes. "Why would they do that?"

"Not even the Russians in the village want the job. Only your mother could put up with that woman."

"My mother never questions her decisions."

"But your mother doesn't cook what she asks for," Anja said.

Mikhel raised one eyebrow at Anja. "Mother makes it look like that good food she has cooked is *exactly* what the Ligacheva asked for. Mother knows how to fight without fighting."

Anja pursed her lips. "What would your mother do if the Ligacheva insisted on what she wanted?"

Mikhel tried to breathe deeply, but his whole side grabbed at his ribs and made him sweat. He knew if pushed, his mother would cave in and just make what was requested. But now, she might over-salt it.

Anja continued. "I heard the Ligacheva screaming at her husband that she was a party member as much as he, and should be able to beat those who disobeyed orders. She said, 'If Leader Brezhnev can remove anti-communists, I can remove these sly Estonians from our own house.'"

"What was she beating you for?"

"I touched the piano again."

"Touched?" Mikhel asked.

"Well, played a little Scarlatti."

"Oh, Anja. You played the sonata that Sergey tries to learn."

She glared at her sleeve cuff.

"Didn't you?"

She looked him in the eye. "He is …"

"He hates music," Mikhel finished. "His mother wants him to seem smarter than everyone else, but he just wants to be in the military like his uncle and his grandfather."

She stared at Mikhel. "How do you know that?"

Mikhel tried to turn his head toward her. "We talk."

Silence from her.

"In the stables, when he's cleaning his horse and I'm cleaning the stalls, we talk."

"But he is always so snobby, just because his father is manager."

"He acts the way his mother has taught him. So do I. And so, Anja, do you."

She backed away from him. "I don't act like my mother. She's mean and stingy and bossy."

"I've heard your mother taunt people in town with her ability to handle the fine dishes and furniture of the manor. Playing the Scarlatti in front of Sergey's mother, isn't that taunting?"

"You're making out that he's the good guy and I'm the evil one."

"What is good, my Anja? What is evil?"

"Just because you are five years older than me, that doesn't make you the wise one."

"You are right. If I were very wise, I would have found a better way to stop Sergey's mother."

"Sergey's been practicing since that day, but very loud."

Mikhel smiled at her. Smiling tightened a band of inflamed muscles around his head, but he said, "You can sing the Scarlatti. I've heard you."

"What? You don't make sense."

"Sing with Sergey. He'll get a kick out of it."

"You're nuts."

"He says you're the only one who ever stands up to his mother. He says that's only because you're more curious than smart, but he likes that you do it."

"I'm smart."

"Smart enough to make friends with Sergey?"

"Sergey's old enough for college. He won't want to be friends with a ten-year-old."

"How many friends do you see here for Sergey?"

She waved her hand at the whole manor landscape.

"Right," Mikhel said. "All the old guys that work for his father and all the young kids. The ones his age have gone to the city to find work."

"Why don't they send him to school in Tallinn."

"Don't know. Ask him." Mikhel closed his eyes.

Anja said, "They'll beg your mom to come back. Uncle Jarve tells her to raise her price."

Mikhel opened his eyes. "Why is that danged music box so important?"

"Don't know. Ask them."

His eyelids drooped again.

She said, "It's gone anyway."

He looked at her. "Who took it?"

"The servant. Sergey's mother beat the cranking arm off it and made him take it to the cellar before her husband saw it."

Mikhel tried to take a deep breath, but it hurt his chest, so he just closed his eyes. As he drifted off to sleep, he thought about the music box.

It's basically ugly. It doesn't work. But it scares people, or at least it scares her. I wonder why?

Days later, Anja came back with an enormous black book. She sat in a chair with the book covering her lap.

"I will read to you from *Kalevipoeg*."

"Where did you find that. It's not supposed to be studied."

"Uncle Jarve put a new cover on it so no one will know."

She wrestled with the large book and then spoke. "Did you know," Anja said with what seemed very practiced off-hand manner. "Did you know that Sergey can also sing and wishes to join the adult's choir?"

"But we sing in Estonian."

"He can sing in Estonian. He says he listens to your mother and learns from her."

"What do you think we should do?"

"We should ask Mrs. Jannsen and Mr. Ivar. Now I will read."

Mikhel lay back and let the sound of her voice wash through him with stories of the giant son of Kalev. In his pain, he began to recognize a new Anja. Anja, ten years old, a nice singing voice, an ability to read rhythm and rhyme as story, and make sense of the old adventures conjured from Estonian stories and tales heard by Frederick Reinhold Kreutzwald so many years ago.

How was this the Anja he had tried to protect, the Anja who let no one protect her as she fought those with power? Was she really changing, or did he merely hope that was what he heard as she read?

The son of Kalev celebrated some successful battle against northern invaders. As Kalev hurled stones and got very drunk, Mikhel allowed himself to sleep.

When he awoke, he found the book propped on his bed and Anja asleep in the chair. He looked more closely at her and realized, unbelievable as it seemed, she had fallen asleep crying.

After his few minutes of quiet wonder, her Uncle Jarve came into the room. He took in the scene, gathered the book to the dresser top and then lifted Anja from the chair. He nodded to Mikhel and left. Mikhel tried to sit up, to get to the book, but he couldn't leave the bed.

An hour later, Jarve returned. "Do you want to read more?" he asked.

"Yes."

Jarve brought the book to his bed and let it rest against Mikhel's chest.

"She was crying," Mikhel said.

"She knows she was the cause, yet she ran away."

Mikhel could only look at Jarve Saarela. After a moment, Jarve sat in the chair.

"Will I get well?" Mikhel asked.

Jarve nodded. "Slowly, but you will get well."

"Are you and Velo building something?"

Jarve nodded.

A silence followed. Then Jarve said, "We had to move the old piano from Illumagi. They are laying more mines along the coast."

Mikhel understood. The chapel was off limits now. The soviets feared peasants using the coast to leave for those ugly capitalist countries, or worse, to signal capitalist submarines in the Baltic. So, Illumagi became a storage place for more explosives for placement in the forest and on the beach.

"Where is the piano?"

"At the barn."

"But it will die in winter."

"On your grandfather's old farmland, we're building a community house for singing."

So, Mikhel thought, they build far enough from any real farming that the Ligachevs might not hear the Estonian songs. And if they can't be heard, the old folks might even worship there.

"Is Sergey joining the choir?"

Jarve shook his head. "Sergey finally stood toe-to-toe with his mother. He is joining the Army. He leaves for officer training in a few days. But he means to visit you before he goes."

Jarve leaned forward. "You are fifteen, almost sixteen. If you don't get well, they won't take you into the army."

Mikhel felt his head become hot and tears form. "But I want to get well. And Velo…"

"Yes, he will go into the army soon. The Soviets still choose to shoot villagers in Afghanistan."

Afghanistan: the hell that sent men and boys home maimed, either outside or inside.

"If you get well, you can learn how to shape a keel for the sleigh."

"A sleigh has a keel?"

"Ours will have two, but we will call them runners."

Mikhel watched Jarve watch him. All those bent-wood boxes in the garden, the caulking lessons, the lessons in how to draw a pattern on the woodshop floor from a list of dimensions – all was leading to something Jarve wanted him to understand, but he had been too young to understand until this moment.

Suddenly, he feared Jarve prepared to leave them. "Are you building anything by yourself, Mr. Jarve?"

Jarve still watched Mikhel as if to see understanding. "No. Not at this time."

"Before?"

"What I might have built before you and Velo is not relevant. Meaning comes when you learn what you need and are ready to teach it to others."

"I will get well, and I will learn."

"Good. It will help you if you sing. That will build breath and strength."

Mikhel pointed at the *Kalevipoeg*. "Mr. Kreutzwald wrote in rhyme. Are there any songs made from that book?"

Jarve shrugged. "You can find the best of his stories and create your own song. Or your own story."

"I'm no giant."

Jarve leaned forward. "Does that matter? What has the *Kalevipoeg* done that you cannot do?"

"Well, nobody lets me get drunk, yet."

Jarve leaned back and laughed. "He does that. And it gets him into the same muddle-brained troubles that drink gives us all. But what does he do that is heroic?"

"He fights off all enemies and saves his mother, Linda, from capture."

"And these are enemies who invade our land, no?"

"Correct."

"We Eesti do not run off to far lands looking to invade others because we know what a disaster that is."

"True."

"Save our mother from invaders. This," Jarve said, standing up, "is something you and I can do."

He made ready to leave the room, but first he tapped Mikhel on the shoulder. "Breathe, sing, move and get well."

Mikhel lay back, his fingers still on the epic story, but his mind on those who took his grandfather to the east, and Anja's father and so many others.

In his dreams, he saw that the Soviets had created a giant. The tower near Tallinn blasted out radio and television stories about how beautiful life in the Soviet countries had become. Mikhel knew that at least in Estonia, this was a lie, except, perhaps for the lives of the cooperative-farm manager and his wife.

And the tower broadcast stories of the enemy, The North Atlantic Treaty Organization and the Americans. What is truth? He wondered, and what is a lie from their giant?

* *

Sergey came when Mikhel was moved to his home. Mother hovered nearby until Mikhel asked her to bring them cookies. That way, she knew he trusted Sergey.

Sergey pulled up his pant legs slightly as he sat in the chair, a habit he had from trying to keep his pants creased neatly.

"You are about to have a uniform, I hear."

"Yes, officer training near Narva."

"You will be posted to Afghanistan?"

Sergey bit his lip. "I might not see you again," he said.

Mikhel studied him silently. After a moment, he said, "That is true, but I hope it is not the way."

"I am sorry for what my mother did to you."

"I know. You would not do such a thing."

"Nor my father."

"No."

"Thank you for your friendship," Sergey said.

Mikhel nodded, tears threatening. "I hope we can be friends again, someday."

Sergey started to say more, but Mikhel's mother brought them cookies and tea. After that, they talked about taking care of Sergey's horse and about Sergey's hope to sing in the Russian army choir.

When he had gone, Ivar came into the bedroom. "A good boy, Sergey," he said.

Mikhel turned his face into his pillow, but he felt his father's hand on his shoulder for a moment before he left the room.

* *

By the time Mikhel was able to walk again, the Ligacheva had rehired his mother at greater expense.

By the time he was able to use a cane and walk to their one-room school, Anja had become a much quieter person. She never argued with her mother. She no longer teased her Uncle Jarve about his woodworking messes or his funny garden boxes. She no longer asked questions that the teachers did not want to answer or could not answer. She brought his books, his lunch, his cane even before he knew he needed them.

On the way home from school, one afternoon, Mikhel stopped in the middle of the path.

"What is wrong with you?" he asked her.

She looked up at him from beneath her bangs, a look that seemed worried and frightened. "I'm fine," she whispered.

"No, you're not. You're a ghost. That math problem the teacher did wrong, you knew it was wrong, but you never said a word."

"I didn't want to cause trouble."

"So, you let a lie sit there on the black board and you let other people think it is the truth?"

"You didn't say anything, so I thought, it must be okay to leave it."

"I never pointed out wrongs before, why would I do it now?"

"Maybe you have always been right not to bug people."

She didn't look him in the eye, so he asked, "Why does my silence seem okay to you?"

She glanced at his cane and said, "Poking at people causes trouble. I get into trouble all the time for doing it."

"But the way you are now, that's not you."

She glanced up at him, tears hovering in her eyes. "I nearly got you killed by taunting her."

He leaned on his cane and said, "No you didn't. I nearly got me killed by playing with the music box. She nearly killed me, not you."

Now, she cried silently.

"Anja," he said.

She sobbed. "I caused it all."

"Anja, I need to sit."

"Oh!" she said, casting about. "There's a rock. Ten feet. Can you...?"

"I can," he said, and hobbled toward the rock where he sat in a sudden collapse. She hovered around him, until he said. "Sit."

She sat in the grass nearby.

"How old are you now?" he asked.

"I'm eleven."

He glanced at her. "So, I missed your birthday."

She nodded.

"I guess I missed mine, as well. I've got to be sixteen if you're eleven."

She smiled. "You aren't sixteen until next month, silly."

That was what he wanted.

"There," he said. "That's good. You can still argue with me."

"Well, you aren't authority."

"Let's make a deal," he said. "I will learn how to be you and speak truth to the teachers and managers. You learn how to be more like me and hold it in. But when it's really important, we will both speak truth."

She stared at him. "You mean it?"

"Yes. Let's go back to the school and I will tell that math teacher he made an error."

"You?"

He thought about the effect on the teacher. "Well, tomorrow. I'll hand him a note, not call him out in front of all the students. We'll see what he does about it."

"Really?"

"You'll see tomorrow."

*   *

That afternoon at the woodshop, Anja sat on a bench and watched the proceedings before they left for choir practice. Velo crawled about on the floor as Mikhel read the dimensions of their next project. Jarve sat next to Anja as she pet the labrador who had followed them in from the nearby farm house.

As they finished up, she stood to see the design they put on the floor.

"Oh," Anja whispered. "A sailboat."

Jarve looked at her and said, "That is a runner for a sleigh."

She looked at him. He leaned down and stared into her eyes.

She shrugged. "A runner for a sleigh may have many uses," she said.

"It may," he said, and he turned toward the boys. "We have choices to make. A sleigh with two runners, a sleigh with one runner and caulking in all the seams, these give us the opportunity to stay or go other places."

The boys stared at him. Anja stood next to him studying all of them.

"Or," Jarve said, "We can choose to stay and find ways to change everything that is wrong. We must figure out how to create openings for change, and how to know when it is time to leave."

Velo pointed at the pattern and said, "I want to make jigs for all these curves, and at the same time, learn to become an announcer at an Estonian radio station."

Anja whispered, "I want to build this sleigh runner, and I will write an Eesti poem of the sea and singing."

Mikhel said, "I want to build a bigger water-tight box to fit this sleigh. And I will show you the choir piece I wrote for *Kalevipoeg* while I recovered."

"And," Jarve said, "I hope we will all be able to sing together for the rest of our days."

Please Remove The Asterisk

My brother takes care of me. I have never been able to walk, and when we were small, Mom and Dad taught Joe how to open my wheelchair. Later he was strong enough to push my wheelchair. He learned how to repair the wheels and brakes on my chair.

Next, he learned how to repair the motor on our car, and that made it possible for him to learn how to repair the motor on my wheelchair. He never realized that by repairing these things while I was with him, I also learned how to repair them. Joe has no idea how many times I've fixed the faulty timing on our ancient Buick.

Joe is now twenty-six and he's never married. I am eighteen. So, we're both adults now. Joe has had girlfriends. But he never asked any of them to marry him. Why? Because of me.

I want to have girlfriends, myself, but that is not happening. Not as long as Joe is nearby.

Joe is my transportation. He is my financial advisor, and it appears he intends to be my 'domestic partner'.

But I want love.

I find this situation totally unhappy, and up to this point, I can't tell Joe.

And then today, I heard a lawyer talk on the radio. She talked about family as more than the usual: more than Mom and Dad and two kids; more than mom and kids from various fathers; more than two lesbians who can finally get married, or two families blending.

She talked about sitting down with all the oddly configured families and ironing out expectations. What does he want? What does the other one want? How can we come up with an agreement that allows us all to be the family we really need to have?

I called her office. I made an appointment. Now, all I have to do is get Joe there.

We are two brothers stuck together by a wheelchair and parents who were wonderful, but then died and left us feeling obligations.

Don't mistake me. I love Joe. I appreciate Joe. But I don't want Joe and me to grow old together without other adventures.

So, tonight, at dinner.

*   *

Joe comes home from the auto-repair shop and discovers I'm making dinner.

"What are you doing, Dylan? You'll burn yourself."

"Haven't burned me yet," I say, continuing to chop carrots. "I'm using the new Insta-pot."

"Here," he says, trying to take my knife. "Let me do that."

"I'll stab you if you try that again. Just let me do, Joe. I don't particularly like hamburger and spaghetti sauce every night."

"But you'll cut…"

"Yes, I will. So back off, please."

"What has gotten into you?"

"I realized that I can do things you've never thought I could do. I can do them even if the countertops are too tall for me and even if the sink faucet is unreachable. I can do them, so I'm going to learn how to do them."

"But I'm glad to do them," Joe said.

"And I will enjoy doing them, also. We can take turns from now on."

"I can't watch."

"Okay," I said, "Get a beer and read the newspaper or something."

"I hate reading the news."

"Well, you used to play the piano when Mom cooked. You can take that up again."

"When Mom cooked, I wasn't in charge."

"News flash! You are not in charge now."

"I'm your guardian."

"Until I'm an adult. Second news flash!"

"Eighteen is not an adult."

"In this state, it is."

"No! Twenty-one …"

"That was then. This is now. In Oregon, eighteen is an adult. I can choose my friends. I can cook our dinner, and I can sign up for college classes using my trust fund."

Joe stopped and stared … and stared.

"You may need to get a life, Joe," I said. "Because I am not your project anymore."

Joe sat.

"Wanta beer?" I asked.

"Wanta figure what's gotten into you."

"Okay, I'll let you come with me to the counselor. I've made an appointment for this coming Monday after four p.m.. Downtown. I'll take the bus. You can come, too. I invite you."

"Counselor? What the hell for?"

"That's where I'm going to figure out what the hell for. I will talk to this person about what I want out of life beyond being in a wheelchair."

"I thought we had a good thing going here. Aren't we brothers? Aren't we chugging along pretty good?"

I said, "Joe, we are chugging along, but I want more. Maybe you want more too. Come with me Monday and let's figure out what more there is to want."

*   *

Six Mondays later, we stepped out of that counselor's office. I rolled down the hall to the nearest sofa area and Joe followed me.

I just waited.

He sat.

"What do you think?" I asked.

"I'm thinking I should call my boss and ask for a raise and a rise up the ladder."

"Is that really where you want to be working ten years from now?" I asked.

"No. The raise and the rise will let me begin to apply for the jobs I really want."

"What are those?"

"I want to create programs that help governments really know what is going on, instead of thinking they know what is going on by guessing."

I laughed. "You know, Joe. That's kind of what I want to study, but I want to help improve planning for transportation for now, instead of planning for transportation yesterday."

"Don't tell me," Joe laughed. "You've applied to the School for Urban Studies."

"I did. Applied last week."

He slumped in his sofa. "I applied a month ago for the evening only classes. If we get in, how're we going to eat?"

"I start work at Home Depot in June the day after high school graduation."

"Work? Boy you have been planning to take over yourself."

I laughed. "Joe, my brother. I'm not leaving you. We're moving on together."

"Wait a minute," Joe said. "Don't you have a senior party after graduation?"

"Yep, but Janean Storey is getting her dad's car and bringing me home."

"Your wheelchair. . ."

"That car will hold my hand operated wheelchair."

"Hand operated? Better wear your gloves guy."

I looked at my hands where the blisters have left callouses. "I know. I've got Carhart work gloves in the chair seat.

Joe looked at his hands, then back up at me.

"Dylan," he says. "I'm sorry."

"Sorry about what?"

He glances off down the hall. "I'm sorry I never thought about you wanting to be independent and . . . and well you know."

"Me being in love?"

"Yeah. Who is this Janean Storey?"

"Not a love interest. Janean has been my school friend since elementary grades. We talk about architecture and science and how data is used or miss-used to make changes in the world."

"Really? She's a data and science nerd?"

I laughed. "Sure. Data and Science nerd. You got her all pigeon-holed now, eh?"

"Well, that's what you said," Joe huffed.

I decided not to say anything more. Already had the biggest thing I wanted, which was that Joe stop treating me like a project. Next, well we'll see what comes next.

*　*

On June 9th, the night after graduation, Janean Storey comes to the house for the first time since about fourth grade. In fourth grade, Janean sported a lot of knee and elbow scrapes and a full set of teeth braces.

At eighteen, Janean is this leggy girl with a long dark ponytail. She is our star basketball player on the women's team. She's also the main striker on the women's high school soccer team. She's the reason our high school women's soccer team went to state. She is all these things because she knows how to divvy up her time between study and play. She also knows where to be on any field to get her hands or her feet on the ball and send that round thing to the right place.

But what Janean really has become is my lab partner in science and my seat partner in calculus, because what the other guys don't know is that most of my science and math four points are the result of studying on the phone and in the library with Janean.

Guys see Janean, and all they register is style and shape. And they pant after what they see. What they don't get a clue about is Janean's mind. I love style and shape, but I've got a real bead on Janean's mind. And Janean's mind has been important to my becoming the guy I am – an independent thinker and a guy with a goal. Janean is the sister I needed to push me off the depression I might have had. In sixth grade, when I couldn't play most sports, it was Janean who got into a wheelchair and started racing me.

I should have told Joe about that long ago, but I didn't. She wins those races, but she is the only one who does. I can now beat almost all other comers.

So, up drives Janean and Joe sees style and shape and I can tell he is struck good.

But Janean just opens the door to let me transfer into the front seat and then she folds up my wheelchair, hoists it into the truck. Janean says, "Bye, Joe. We'll be back about midnight."

The party was great. I danced with girls I wanted to dance with and would never see again, but we had a good time and when things were winding down, Janean and I got into her dad's Chevy and trundled on home.

The best part, however, was the sideways grilling that I got from Joe during the next weeks.

"Did you and Janean have a good time?" He couldn't bring himself to ask the question directly.

"Sure."

"Is Janean going to Portland State, too?"

I thought, *don't you hope...* but I said. "Not that I know of." I knew danged well that she was taking pre-med at the Catholic university in North Portland. I knew she would be in town, where if he made an effort, he could find her, but I also knew he was never going to ask me for her telephone number. So, I dangled him in his misery.

*   *

The day after the graduation party I took the bus to the Home Depot on Columbia Street. At Home Depot, I noticed that when I signed in, there was an asterisk next to my name.

"What's that there for?" I asked.

Mrs. Duncan, the lady at the newcomers' desk, looked at that flashing star and said, "That's to remind the supervisor that you are in a wheelchair."

"What does that mean to the supervisor?"

"It means, don't ask you to climb a ladder and haul down a box full of toilets."

I said, "Good plan. But what does it tell the supervisor that I can do?"

She shrugged. "I guess it tells him you can do anything that can be reached from a chair."

"Fair enough."

But my supervisor was not so sanguine about having me as a worker. "From there, you can't even reach the faucets and the screw drivers. What the hell am I supposed to do with you?"

"Is that the customer relations training?" I asked.

Clearly, that was not a joke to this man.

"Customer relations is being able to show people where things are. Can you even see things higher than the third shelf?"

"Let me put on my reading glasses so I can see things closer than the ceiling," I said, and by then I was expecting him to realize I might be jacking him.

Instead, he waited for me to produce the glasses. So, I said. "Shelf four, drill bits of various sizes, some in packages that give you most of the reasonable sizes, some by themselves so the customer can buy only the one he needs at this time."

He said, "Encourage the package deal."

"Even if it is not what the customer needs?"

"You want this place to make money?"

"Ah, the customer relations training. I get the drift." I said.

"What could you know about building trades? You can't be a help to customers who want to know how to do things."

"I've been getting ready for this job by YouTubing all kinds of building projects."

"Gotta have hands on experience. I don't know what you think you can do in this environment. Why don't you get a job at Macy's or some such place?"

"Ah, sir, I would never have the chance at Macy's to learn from a professional such as you."

He backed up. "Well," he said, "You are certainly going to learn."

He left me there in the aisle. I pinned on my employee badge and started wheeling down the aisle, figuring out what materials might be in each shelf and how it might help a homeowner or a builder.

Ten minutes later, I was in the third aisle from where I started when a customer came up to me and asked, "Where can I find the rings you use to seat a toilet?"

"Good afternoon," I said. "I'm Dylan Travis. Those are in Aisle twenty-seven, but let me tell you about a new way to seat a toilet that will be less likely to leak or move."

"Okay. I have only used the rings a couple of times, and I don't find them at all easy to seat. I'm Michael, by the way."

Another five minutes and Michael is on his way with the new toilet seating kit with a silicon ring when the supervisor comes back.

He says, "I got you transferred to the garden shop. That's stuff you can reach from down there."

"Really," I said. "Let me ask you about seating a toilet."

"Buddy, you aren't going to be able to do that from there."

"True, but how is it done?"

"You get this ring – a beeswax ring, from over in aisle, oh, I think it is aisle twenty-two."

"What about a silicon ring?" I asked.

"That's an untried and expensive marketing toy. You want the tried method. Worked for years."

"How do I get to the garden center and who is my supervisor there?"

"Out here, to the right and off to the other end of the store."

I wheeled out and went to the main office. Mrs. Duncan, the lady who hired me was there.

She said, "Dylan, what can I do for you?"

"My supervisor just told me to go to the garden center because I could reach things in that department. Who is the supervisor over there?"

She put her papers down on her desk. "Who told you to go there?"

"I believe his name is Dan. That's what his nametag said, but he didn't introduce himself, so I don't know what his last name is."

She held out a piece of paper and said, "Read this."

"I took it and saw that it was signed *Michael Bolen*. It said, "Customer commendation for Dylan Travis. This salesperson knows his stuff and offered great advice."

I looked up at her. "That's very nice of him."

"Doesn't happen very often," she said. "The garden supervisor is Gail Verde. She'll love having you. Know anything about plants?"

"Only the ones that grow around my house, but I'll learn the new ones."

"I'm sure you will. Let me walk down there and introduce you to her."

"Thank you, Mrs. Duncan."

*   *

Three days later, I started school at the Urban Studies department of Portland State University. My first visit to my counselor, I saw my papers on her desk. There was an asterisk next to my name.

I thought I knew the answer even as I asked, "What does the asterisk mean?"

She glanced at the paper and said, "It means you are in a wheelchair and should have classes where the elevator or the ramps can take you."

"Oh. But it doesn't mean I need things made easy for me, right?"

"Right. It just means you need to be where you can get out in case of an emergency."

"Ah. That makes sense."

After our talk about what to take and how to plan my four years, I left her office and I thought, 'there must be a way to get wheelchairs to all the floors of this building.'

By the time I had my grades for the first quarter, I also had learned a hundred new plants in Home Depot's garden section. I learned where they live best and what they need to thrive. When Dan Whats-his- face was off the floor, I also perused the aisles for home repair needs so I could tell customers where things were and what they might want.

*   *

For weeks, Joe persisted in testing the Janean connection, trying to fathom my feelings about her and also hoping to connect with her when he found we really were just friends. About her phone, I gave him nothing.

Joe kept working at the auto repair shop, where he now was the night manager. He started school at Portland State in the mornings and then went home to sleep and study in the afternoons. The guy was wearing out. So, I looked up scholarship possibilities and took some advice about our trust funds from Mom and Dad's old friend and lawyer.

Joe is stubborn, so I held my fire until he truly would listen.

*   *

From Portland State University, I took a bus that passed one of our city's many hospitals. The first time I got on, the bus driver helped me tie into the wheelchair opening at the side of the bus. He said, "You want off at Emmanuel Hospital?"

"No, sir. I'm headed home to Thirty-second Avenue."

"I can let you off at Fremont and Thirty-second."

I knew that area, of course. I live there. Thirty-second is nearly the top of a long hill – a side moraine of rock and debris left to us by the many Missoula Floods back in the years minus fifteen to twelve thousand. My house is on the back side of that moraine, in the lowland swept out by the floods as they went by.

I said, "Heck of a downhill ride to Siskiyou Street. How about drop me at Twenty-eighth? A slower hill. Better for my brakes."

"Sounds good to me."

Now, when I get on, the guy, Charles Wright, asks, "How is college going?"

"Pretty darned good, Charlie. Project on improving transportation this week."

"Yeah?"

"What ideas have you got?" I ask. And we're off with me learning more about city transportation than I can keep track of. Like, for instance, how good it is if you want to come from the out-lands into the city, but how hard it is to get from north to south on any side of town without first going into the city and transferring out again to someplace that is only two or three miles south or north of where you started.

Sometimes, I talk to folks downtown and gather ideas for a project that Joe's night class is doing. We came to that agreement one afternoon when I told Joe all about what I learned from Charlie Wright, the bus driver.

Joe gets ideas for me. It's a good trade.

At the office of Portland State University, the asterisk bothered me. But I was in a wheelchair and did need emergency escape possibilities. So, I let it ride – so to speak.

One day, I tied myself into the wheelchair station on the bus. At the next stop, the girls from St. Mary's Catholic High School piled onto the bus as they usually did after school.

I know from experience that they are on for the ride to the Nordstrom's outlet store. On this day, they gaggle and laugh and don't move back. They are a party in search of a place to spend money. They are loud.

Charlie pulled up to the next bus stop and let a young lady in an office suit on. She could only get as far as the lowest step.

Charlie said, "Girls, please move to the back and make room for new passengers."

They didn't hear him.

I tried to help. "Ladies, the bus driver is asking you to make room by moving back."

They didn't hear me.

I reached out and touched the arm of the nearest girl. She jumped, stared at me and recoiled. I knew that touching her was a mistake.

I said, "The bus driver asked you all to move back and make room for other passengers."

She stared at me without seeming to hear what I said. "Don't take advantage," she whines.

I repeated, "The bus drivers said move back. Make room."

"Don't touch me."

Charlie pulled up to the next bus stop. A man in a tee shirt, torn overalls and wearing long and very greasy ponytail and a very grimy backpack stood at the corner. He couldn't get on because of the girls in the stairwell and on down the aisle.

He hollers at Charlie. "Let me on."

The young lady on the bottom step explained. "The bus driver asked the girls to move back, but they can't hear him."

The grimy fellow says "Ma'am, could you step off and let me on? I'll show you how to change that situation."

She smiled and stepped off. He rose into the lowest step and shouted. "Ladies. If you don't move, I'm coming through, and I'll drop my cooties all over you."

The girls nearest him screamed. "Move back. Move back!"

The whole crowd of girls suddenly dissolved toward the back of the bus. The man turned to the young lady. "I believe you can get on now," he said. Then he looked at me and said, "There is more than one way to skin a cat."

"I now believe it." I laughed.

Charlie said, "Tom, here's a month's pass for you, sir."

"Why thank you. Appreciate it." And Tom took the bus pass and shoved it into his overall pocket. Then he beckoned the young lady onto the bus.

"Tom Laughlin at your service, Ma'am."

"I am Lisa Weatherman," she said. "Thank you for an enlightening lesson in crowd control."

They laughed together and then amazed me when they took a seat together across from me. And by the time she disembarked, he had her laughing about life.

When she was gone, he turned to me and said, "No real cooties, here. Just the usual vermin. And that is one nice lady."

"I believe that, too."

The girls from St. Mary's still got on the bus every day after school, but they all moved to the back right away.

Since then, I've noticed that Lisa, the young lady, seemed to wait at Tom's bus stop instead of hers before she got on to go home. They always had a great conversation for about six miles. And every week, he became a little bit less grimy, while she looked a bit less spiffy.

One day, after Lisa got off, Tom leaned over to me. "I have a job."

"That's great."

"Yup. Funniest part is I do the cleanup in the back room at Nordstrom's Rack, you know? Their resale store. You can't believe the mess those girls leave on the floor."

"Doesn't surprise me."

"Privilege does that to you. Makes you leave others to clean up after you."

"Yes," I said. I started then, thinking about the messes I might leave because I am privileged. I have had loving mom and dad, and a great brother and now this chance to go to college on a trust fund. What messes have I left?

And what I've seen from those two bus riders is that there is hope for love from a wheelchair as well.

*   *

Speaking of messes, I left Janean's email address on the breakfast table. It was supposed to look like an accident, but of course it wasn't.

I knew Joe wanted to see her more. I thought I'd made it hard for him for too long. Later, I wished I had left her report card there too, but I didn't. And now, he's writing back and forth with her, maybe twice a week. At first, he sent a mass text like "How's college going for all of you this year?" and he included two or three of my guy friends.

She answered a reply to him plus me. He answered the same way. And then, they were off on their own, without intermediaries. And for some reason, I'm afraid he won't get her mind when all he might be thinking about is shape and style.

Of course, I like Janean's shape and style, too, but we've been friends for so long that I don't get what you might call smitten. She's important, but it's not love. I just don't want somebody else to misunderstand what she is worth.

*   *

At school, I've met some very nice girls, and I find there are several who actually talk to the guy in the wheelchair as if he were just another guy. I'm not in love with anybody, but I can see that there is a future for me somewhere with some girl. So, I stick to business and hope she will appear on my horizon one day,

*   *

And then, one afternoon, Janean Storey came over to our house. We were all sharing a beer when suddenly Janean began crying. It turns out that her pre-med professor had suggested she join the nursing class at her college. He said she was wasting her talents on becoming a pediatrician.

"How old is this guy," Joe asked her. He didn't put an arm around her, like I thought he would. Instead, he handed her a tissue.

She took it and answered, "He's maybe forty."

"Huh!" Joe said. "Young enough to know better. Is he intimidated by you?"

"Intimidated?" She looked really perplexed.

"Is he afraid you are smarter than him?" Joe asked.

"Well, I get As in all my science classes."

"Thought so," Joe said.

And there was amazed me, sitting there thinking Joe didn't get her. A lot I know.

"Janean," he said. "You just keep on keeping on. This guy will be a part of your past soon. He'll be stuck revving his engines, and you will be a pediatrician. You go, girl."

Revving his engines? I thought. Looked to me like Joe had been working with cars too long. He needed to get a better vocabulary for talking to girls.

But Janean had other views. "Revving!" she said, between fits of laughter. "That's a good one. And pretty much describes how he teaches – straight from the curriculum – no asides, no interesting stories about his experiences in medicine, no jokes and no laughs and no sadness."

Joe laughed too. "Well, feel sorry for the guy. You will be a much more interesting teacher and are going to be leading students around your hospital while he is still trying to absorb old news in medicine without any idea that he might have been creating new ideas."

*   *

Since that day, I've been very glad Joe has discovered the real Janean. I saw they would be good for each other. So, I sent Janean my research on scholarships for Joe.

As a result of her encouragement, next September Joe will enter the daytime school at Portland State University – the school of urban studies. And he will be studying computer technology as well, so that he can put his ideas about data gathering for problem solving in cities into good use. Soon, he'll be able to show city governments what really works in data gathering, how to interpret what they get and what they don't yet get, and how to see what needs to be tweaked to work better.

I'm pretty sure at some point in the future, we'll be partners working on the solution to some problem that will help Janean's patients kick some disease that attacks children. Or we'll all figure how to get better medicine and services to people in fragile situations.

I've been working about eight hours a week at Home Depot. Gail teaches me about plants. She once said, "Dylan, you're more interested in knowing the merchandise than most."

That surprised me. "Who is not interested in plants and how they live?"

"City kids who never have a chance to grow anything until they have a lawn to mow."

"You know, Gail," I said. "I really enjoy the plants, but my work with Urban Studies means that it would be most helpful if I learned more about building techniques."

"Urban needs include places for people to rest with nature," she said. "Those places are called parks."

I got it. And I'm taking that back to my next project. I think we can figure out how to get more people to and into parks on public transportation. And once we're in there, I bet we can help people appreciate and understand more about what they have in nature.

Meanwhile, I went into the main office and had a talk with Mrs. Duncan, the lady who had hired me.

"Mrs. Duncan, you know that nice note that Michael Bolen left about me?"

"Yes," she said, "Did you know that was only the first of several notes thanking you?"

That took me by surprise. I hadn't heard about these other notes. But I went ahead with my request to her.

"That asterisk next to my name . . ."

"Yes, about the wheelchair."

"Could we take that off my papers?"

She sat back. "You know, I don't think that wheelchair has slowed you down a bit. I'm willing to white out the asterisk and put "Star employee" in its place."

I laughed. "That's great. Thanks."

*   *

In the meantime, the good Charlie Wright drives my chariot to and from classes. Tom and Lisa become closer each day and I won't be surprised if the girls from St. Mary's learn how to clean up after themselves by the time they grow up.

Tom has become the floor manager at Nordstrom's Rack and Lisa is their chief bookkeeper.

Maybe when they figure out how important they are to each other, Tom and Lisa will invite all those girls to the wedding, seeing as how St. Mary's girls were the reason that he and Lisa met.

And me? I'm waiting for love, but I know it will come my way. I no longer feel the asterisk hanging over my wheelchair.

That Girl Down Here

We heard them calling her summat like *Persephone*. They say she was Greek, the girl kid of Demeter, the Goddess of the Harvest.

We seen our God, Pluto, do it. He went and stole this girl during the harvest. And he brought her down here to this dark underbelly of the world.

Her mom must have been looking after the wheat and grape workers at the time.

Really that Persephone never shoulda been down here. Ever. But things ain't always just, if you know what I mean.

I mean, actually, the girl acted refined, ya see? A lady she was, through all them goings on. I do admire that. Yes, I do. But it got her no points with them that count. In the end, I believe being 'ladylike' got her where she is today. Just my own personal thought, but I do rightly believe it.

Like she's in this absolutely lugubrious place and nobody's tellin' her nothing. They don't even give her the time of day. They keepin' her in the dark about should she ever again expect to eat. And they for certain-sure ain't telling that girl about no rules. And there she is kidnapped and hidden in this backwater dive, scared, homesick and starving.

So, the girl sees us and what's she supposed to do? There we are, just set out on that table in her room – and believe me, we been put there in as plain sight as you can get in bad lighting. And it's not like we was a scarce item. Huh-uh! No way! There are thousands of us, like . . . thousands. I mean we were like numerous. Who'd have thought that her jailer was keeping track of us.

And you know yourself that we can tempt the holiness out of a pious stick. I mean – we glisten. We shine. We got colors to put Iris to shame. Mediterranean bright blue, a little hint of red and the gleam of gold.

And juicy? Hummm-uhmm! I mean after all, the girl had got to eat.

So, she taken this one timid bite out of me – hardly a scratch of her pearly whites. I mean she barely got any of me in those dainty little teeth. Six little bitty seeds she ate, and next thing – Whamo – the girl has been tried and convicted. Condemned to live in this low-life place for six months of every year through all eternity.

I mean where is the justice? It was Blind. It was Deaf. And it was gone out to shoot craps – That's justice for you. Plus, get this, they make her become the wife of the dude who stole her in the first place. Pluto, his name was – and I'm here to tell you this fellow was moody. Not the bridegroom du jour, if you know what I mean. He was like Morbid piled on top of the Blues. And well-named, if you ask me. That man was a real dog.

I Will Tell You A Juicy Story

So! B. Franklin, you lovely golden-eyed bird, I see you up there – top of the fir tree. You possibly think I'm lying here in the grass, pawing the air because I dream of chasing rabbits – chasing squirrels and chasing rodents, as you do, Great Hunter.

You want to hear the truth? You want should I tell you the down and dirty? All right. All right. I'm telling you.

It's like this, Franklin, my all-seeing, feathered friend. I am lying here, planning revenge. Wait. Don't get your tail- feathers up. It is not revenge against your recent pranks. Nah, Nah – on my honor as a fellow hunter.

I plan against my nemesis. And this much I promise you. I will have satisfaction. And I will have it big. A revenge among revenges.

You see, it is like this. In this house where I get my food and an occasional walk – when and if they remember that I like a good walk, which for the most part they do not remember – in this house there is a demon. Two years ago, he was put on this earth to torment. He was brought forth in order to make my life a trial. I am the Job of canines.

Pull my ears? Nothing. Wrap my tail around the door handle? A trifle. Ride me like a horse, wearing spurs? – an everyday occurrence.

And get this, Frank, my fine bright-eyed friend – this demon cannot be exorcised. He will not be cast into swine.

Why not, you ask? I tell you this. It is because he is the son. He is the beloved of his father. And, of course, his mother has plans that he will be a doctor, or better, do a Start-Up.

So for her, of course, he does no wrong.

And besides all these expectations, he excites cooing. "Too Cute," his aunties call him. So what earns the little stinker this elevated assessment?

He has curls. Truly. That is it – the whole of his claim to their admiration.

I do not kid you.

Curls, it is. Soft and downy, like lining for the most elegant nest. His grandmother mentions them every visit. All the time, his aunties want to put their hands on them. All the females in his life coo about them – the curls, and the dark brown eyes, and the fat dimples.

No, I swear by your shiny beak, it is the whole truth.

Now I have dimples, myself, you know. But they are beneath my whiskers, so these idiots see nothing. And I have a nice wavy pelt back there near my tail – you can see that for certain. But the whole crowd ignores my curls.

And my eyes, look at my eyes, Frank. Do I not have eyes as big and brown as any you have seen? Any other household and these eyes would bring admirers to their knees.

But among these think-nots, all they see is little curly locks with his dimpled, evil grin.

I tell you a secret. But Frank, you must swear by your enormous wingspan that you will never tell anyone else. This small demon has one other quality that brings him the high regard of every member of the family.

It is his fat. Indeed. Fat is his most charming feature. He has such sausage arms and tender legs. His toes alone would be fit morsels for a king.

You do not believe me? Hover nearby. Yes, that's it. Closer even, and you will see for yourself how he is. In a few moments, the little demon will awaken from his nap. He will bound out the door and be upon me long before his nanny catches up with him. Then you will believe the truth, even from my poor mouth.

Ach. You hear the slam of the screen door? He comes.

You see? Have you ever set eyes upon such a tender morsel? Take a closer look.

Ah! You have seen how tasty.

Quick, Frank. The nurse opens the door already.

Get him off me.

Yes. Hold fast to the little nappy. He cannot harm you with his squeals and kicking. That's the idea. Nah, nah, nah. Don't worry. Go.

Flap those enormous wings and teach the fat one to fly.

Visit again, one day, my sharp-eyed friend.

And now, Frank, thanks to you, I will have that dream. I am chasing rabbits, and they are thumping slow. Awkward bunnies of the first order.

My whole life will now be one dream of peace.

I pay no attention to the shrieking nanny.

An Appetite For Life

Joseph Bruback bent his long, thin body over the woolly cocoon. Gently, he picked it open. With delicate, tweezer-like fingers, he lifted out the worm and placed it on his lab table. It showed no sign of developing wings. Joseph smiled and congratulated the little specimen.

"Well done, fellow. The best yet."

He liked to think that what he had created might bask in his praise. The worm's response, however, was to roll over and hitch its bloated body toward the food tray. Joseph watched it for a moment, and then moved to the next cocoon.

During the development of his worms, Joseph lived for his experiment. He supervised the hatch of each generation of larvae. He loved the constant watchfulness, the puzzle-solving, the outwitting required to change nature. His goal, reduced to simple terms: learn the laws of biology, use the laws to circumvent the laws.

It was an exciting game. Working on a project kept his brain in prime fitness. And to assure that he would never be without scientific conundrums, he kept notes on the best ideas bombarding his consciousness during his sleep deprived state – ideas for subsequent research. He stored his notes in an old-fashioned, three ringed notebook, hidden in his office safe, inside his expensive building, deep in the heart of his famous city.

Because of Joseph's joy in work, his bio-tech company flourished. *Bruback's Deny Laboratories of Chicago* became a recommended stock. Joseph Bruback became a whispered name. His pleasure in experimenting, however, made him oblivious to all else. His colleagues constantly had to re-introduce themselves, even though Joseph had hired them. He barely recognized the other buildings of his great city. He did not notice the people, the conveniences, or the money – only the scientific victories made an impression on his memory.

In the months required for this research, Joseph never left his laboratory. He changed his clothes once a week on Wednesdays when his laundress delivered a new set. Twice daily, he ordered peanut butter sandwiches delivered – noon and midnight. In the four early morning hours, Joseph slept on a train of chairs laid out in couch formation in his office. In the other twenty hours of each day, he burrowed into his work. With these worms he would make a breakthrough of major significance.

He spliced genes. He created cocktails to turn off the normal activities of genes. He tweaked a gene here, and another there. And then he dissected the little grubs so as to understand them better.

One late night, in a close call, his dissecting laser turned on an instant too soon, catching the tip of his finger and then frying the larva that he touched. He washed the contaminating matter from the wound, and treated the finger quickly. No burn or inflammation developed, but he exercised more care afterward. There did seem to be a slight residual effect, perhaps from the adrenaline rush caused by his brush with danger. At the end of the series of experiments, he found it increasingly difficult to focus on his work.

He stared at the burn on his finger, wondering. But he discarded any idea that his focus problems had anything to do with the burn. After all, he had washed it immediately. There could be no larval matter in that finger. The red mark on his finger meant nothing.

Such small difficulties aside, after long, seemingly fruitless months, Joseph successfully created a genetically improved larva. The improvement was that it never self-actualized. It never became the moth it was originally intended to be. It merely went through life eating and growing, weighing more each day until it burgeoned to enormous and unwieldy size. The larva never spun its cocoon, never metamorphosed into the blue and teal creature it might have been. It never flew, nor mated, nor laid eggs for the creation of future generations of moths.

Thus, conveniently arrested in the consuming stage of its life, Joseph's newly developed larva could be transported long distances, stored at low temperatures and sold by the ounce at prices that might eventually put saffron to shame.

In testing his new worm, he was satisfied that it could be replicated by an inexpensive cloning process. He had concocted a solution and developed a centrifuge that spun hundreds of segments of worm until their cells began to divide, divide and divide into complete new worms. Each batch, which originally took two days to create, now could be duplicated in a matter of minutes.

Having achieved economic viability, Joseph ordered a special bottle and then poured himself a finger of Old Turkey Vermouth. He sat on his desk and swirled the Vermouth in his glass. Appreciating the subtle colors and spicy aroma in its fortified liquid, he indulged in a few moments of self-congratulation.

Three minutes of leisure, and then abruptly, he called his chauffeur. After months of creative work, his first excursion into the outer world was to visit his patent lawyer. He stepped out of his building on Wacker Drive, squinting against the brilliant light of day as it reflected off the Chicago River. He felt the sun's heat against his pale skin. Unused to such warmth, he hurried into his Bentley sedan, where the tinted windows helped him recuperate from a feeling of dryness in the skin of his face. He braced himself for the unaccustomed motion of the car as his chauffeur zoomed into traffic and turned right down Wacker Drive toward South Michigan Avenue where Rafael Bunuel, his attorney, maintained an office at a venerable address.

Subsequent to his discussion with Bunuel, Joseph made a side trip, unprecedented for him – a visit to a clothier. In the elegant atmosphere of the famous Paul Stuart on N. Michigan, Joseph looked and smelled quite out of place. His laundered clothes had been donned six days before, and were less than pleasant to others.

Within moments of his entry into the store, however, the Paul Stuart staff recognized the difference between poverty and eccentricity. The doorman, who spotted the Bentley from which Joseph had emerged, gave the dollar sign to the floor man, who passed the news to all levels. Thus, the tailor in the back room willingly pushed aside Don Francis Grazio's evening suit to fulfill the wishes of the ripe gentleman now choosing fabrics of fine wool and extra-virgin silk.

Joseph felt dazed by his own interest in buying. Hitherto, he had very little use for any clothes beyond a weekly clean tee shirt under his lab coat. Nevertheless, an unfamiliar compulsion prodded him into the purchase of five suits, one dark blue tuxedo, ten silk shirts with French cuffs, and all the accessories necessitated by such a wardrobe. He barely knew what those accessories were called or how to attach them to his being.

It seemed to him that he had awakened from a deep sleep where the dreams had all been about science, and now he found himself involved in real life. He knew nothing about how to conduct himself in the purchase of any item designed for his physical pleasure.

The attentions of the Paul Stuart consulting clothiers made him decide to learn this new game as well as he had learned the game of science. He put off the moment when he must leave the pleasurable room and return to his barren laboratory. In fact, he determined that he would not return to the lab, but might instead go on to a restaurant and indulge himself in further pampering.

For this purpose, Joseph changed into one of his new suits, complete with a chartreuse silk shirt, diamond cuff links and lavender Ezio tie with a tromp-l'oeuil print of moonlight and cumulous clouds over the night woods.

When he looked at himself in the three-way mirror, he saw only the brilliant, feverish eyes of a man in a suit, and the billowing, larval shapes upon the tie. Some sick sense brought awareness of how he had misspent today's precious time. Awakening to a vague, lurking danger ended his acquiescence to salesmen. He paid his bill and left the building at once.

On the street, he fought against a renewed urge to enter any clothing store. Urgently cell-phoning his chauffeur, he strode down the street, followed by the box boy of Paul Stuart's, who toted a frightening collection of goods.

Joseph sidled along the avenue between confusing groups of oncoming pedestrians. To his relief, the chauffeur soon pulled to the curb beside him. The man gave him a quizzical glance as the embarrassing boxes were settled into the trunk of the car. Joseph ignored the look. He also repressed the desire of his fingers to caress the label on the last box. Instead, he dove into the passenger seat and let the chauffeur tip the boy.

Once extricated from the apparel district, Joseph meant to regain control over his actions. He directed his chauffeur to return to Deny Labs. When they arrived at the parking garage, he pulled himself from the plush seat of his Bentley. He told his chauffeur to return home and have the maid put away the purchases in whatever attic closet she found. He firmly resolved never to look at them again.

Moving slowly, Joseph forced himself to re-enter the world of science which, until today, had created all his pleasure in life. One excursion to the clothing store had momentarily blunted his taste for the research game. Reviewing his actions, he became convinced that his next purchase would have put him on the wrong side of a precipice, doomed to fall into unknown depths.

Joseph pushed himself, step by step, away from the void and into his lab. Sweating with alarm, he pulled out his notebook, ready to dive into the next idea for research. On each page, he focused and refocused his eyes. He took off his glasses. The words swam up and across the paper. He thrust his glasses back onto his face and turned over another page. Staring at each new leaf, Joseph became more and more confused. He could not believe he'd thought these were good ideas. Understanding individual sentences, even paragraphs, he still could not see that they had significance to him. He tossed the notebook aside.

Convinced he'd worn himself out during his previous labors over the larvae, he recalled his chauffeur and had himself driven home. Once there, he slept, ate and slept again for seventy-two hours.

By the time he awoke fully, he decided he'd been a fool to believe life consisted only of research and scientific triumph. Life outside of his lab had many sensuous experiences to offer. Joseph Bruback determined he would taste each of them. He had his new clothes retrieved from the attic. In accord with this momentous decision, he donned the chocolate *de laine à tricoter* with its delicate stripes of red and blue.

Suitably dressed, he returned to his office long enough to disclose the contents of his notebook to three of his top scientists. Noting the gleam of excitement in each face, he had a momentary longing to join them in their search. The feeling lasted only through the first sentences of the discussion. Once free of the irrational desire to do experiments, he dealt with the division of labor between his colleagues. After leaving them to their idiot delights, Joseph celebrated his liberation from long nights, the bed of hard chairs and the occasional accidents of a modern laboratory. He had grown beyond all that.

The patent that his lawyer, Rafael Bunuel, had now secured for the Deny Power Larva gave Joseph's company the potential for unlimited marketing, and greatly improved his already superior fiscal empire. Carefully advertised as *Wriggle-bits*, the Deny Power Larva became a tasty treat – at first, marketed as pet food – purchased by lovers and collectors of crickets, fish, and exotic birds.

Soon, Joseph's public relations department hired a more creative advertising firm which tapped into an even greater customer base. Up-and-coming executives, who prided themselves on being at the leading edge of a culinary revolution, discovered the erotic texture of *Larguini*, a protein-based pasta. These young pinstriped suits used new communication options to tell their friends of the discovered delicacy. Thus, they provided web-wide distribution to the idea that *Larguini* enhanced the sexual power of those who enjoyed its subtle flavor.

This word of mouth advertising brought about an exponential increase in the value of Joseph's stock. Immediately prior to a peak in the market, Joseph sold significant, but not controlling percentages in Deny Industries to Rafael Bunuel. Joseph thus diversified his portfolio, but retained rights to the Power Larva. He was guaranteed an extraordinary income for the rest of his natural life.

After first becoming aware of all that he'd missed, Joseph bought extravagantly – a three-million-dollar condominium in a renovated building in the depths of Randolph Street. His rooms, now elegantly furnished, faced north, away from the sunlight that continued to bother his sensitive skin. For himself and his growing number of friends, he imported food of the highest quality – food raised on ranches or grown on farms he owned in Wisconsin, Wyoming and Montana.

He chose playmates as committed to the consuming life as he was. They pouted after coats from Elan furriers to cover their sleek bodies, baubles from Collezione di Bergio – gems to make their eyes light up. Each playmate in turn displayed his wealth in lovely, carefully cultivated cool. They represented the ultimate in fine, female art. Of course, after a few months, each one in turn developed flaws – small lines of tension about the eyes and mouth, small pouches lacking tension in a throat or derriere. Each discarded playmate enjoyed a small stipend because Joseph grew too languid to cultivate enemies.

Over the months, *Larguini* came to play a greater and greater part in the diet of everyone he knew. This pleased him, at first. Becoming a culinary connoisseur, he joined them in discovering new ways to serve his creation. Some said *Larguini* far outshone any other protein source for its ability to convey the flavors of its sauces.

Joseph found he had a craving for *Larguini* with chocolate sauce. And during the next years, as a result of his new habits, he evolved into a man of generous proportions. The changes in his girth necessitated frequent visits to his favorite clothier. By the end of the second year, his body had bloated to accommodate his consumption of several pounds of chocolate sauce per week. He did not worry about his size because he continued to attract gorgeous women.

After four years of full-time sensuality, however, Joseph grew bored. He wished for a wife, but no woman who interested him seemed to desire what he desired – children. Attempting to attract a woman who already exhibited mothering qualities, he found himself saying all the wrong things. His little joke about wanting his own team always fell like a deflated basketball. The current object of his desire also took his intended compliments on her obvious mothering equipment as an insult concerning her weight. He could not attract mothers and when he tried to make a mother of any of his playmates, he failed miserably. He seemed to have no aptitude for causing conception.

One evening, as he sipped chocolate sauce through a crystal straw, Joseph took a good look at himself, and then studied the *Larguini* left over from his dinner. He surveyed his life over the five years since his discovery. Gazing at the small red mark on his lasered finger, he came to a conclusion. He needed to return to Deny Laboratories and begin work once again.

But he thought perhaps he would rest a little more before plunging his body into the ordeal of scientific research. That evening, he fell asleep in his deep chair. At two in the morning, his chauffeur gently covered him with a blanket and turned out the light.

*   *

With no wife, no children and no shirt-tail relatives, none noticed that Joseph's fortune grew faster than even a hedonist could spend it – none noticed except his lawyer and investment counselor – Rafael Bunuel.

Rafael loved the game and the business of law. He loved the constant vigilance, the puzzle-solving, the outwitting required to change the nature of property. His motto, in its most succinct form, read: Learn the laws of money, use the laws to circumvent the laws.

It was an exciting game. Working for a client kept his mind in prime fitness. He spent very little time on anything else.

His favorite client was Joseph Bruback: Joseph clearly enjoyed the fruits of Rafael's labors. It was true that once, years ago, Joseph had created money. Several discoveries in his bio-tech labs had yielded great profits. The development of *Larguini* had been a stroke of pure genius. Since the patenting and marketing of that wiggly little gem, however, Joseph had not needed to create money. His money created money. It was almost too easy.

Rafael needed a challenge. He believed that recently Joseph, too, had been showing signs of restlessness, so Rafael guessed he might be ready to return to work in the labs. With a little nudge, Joseph might develop a new product. With a new product, they could create more capital, invest in money-making start-ups, buy property, play the game.

So, one morning Rafael cell-phoned Joseph and invited him to lunch. Having waited until well after sunrise, he was surprised to have found Joseph asleep. Nevertheless, his invitation was accepted.

Then, however, Rafael realized he had a guest coming who was used to perfect food and a perfect ambiance. Gazing around his condominium, he saw that his minimalist, even negligent, decorating was not exactly conducive to convivial entertaining.

Besides, Rafael had never learned to cook anything beyond the occasional fried egg on toast, so he made a quick decision and reserved a table at Valdosti's in Little Italy. At noon, he hurried downstairs to meet Joseph in the vestibule of his condominium.

As usual, Rafael was amazed that such a thin man could become such a corpulent monstrosity. After wedging his client into the passenger seat of his Rolls Royce, Rafael drove them to the restaurant near Roosevelt Road on Halsted Street.

Even at noon, Valdosti's exuded the aromas of mizithra cheese, sweet garlic and mushrooms. After the waiter seated them, Rafael happened to notice that the chef offered an appetizer of *Larguini*-stuffed tomatoes. He thought to honor his guest by ordering this most successful of his creations. Joseph's embarrassed reaction made Rafael certain he had started the meal off on a positive note.

Having never actually eaten *Larguini*, Rafael was not certain how he would ignore the knowledge of what they were. When the plate arrived, the bright color of the baked tomato, combined with the fragrance of perfect Béchamel sauce made him hungry. He ate his share of the appetizer with gusto. The taste seemed to caress his tongue before heating his throat and then his chest.

Across the table, Joseph hesitated long, but at Rafael's encouragement, he succumbed to the wonderful smells. He seemed as surprised as Rafael to enjoy the redolent treat. Rafael ordered a second plate of the appetizer. He began to work his conversation around to a rejuvenation of Joseph's ambitions in the field of science.

But in mid-paragraph, he saw Joseph push away his second tomato. Joseph spoke right through Rafael's sentence.

"Listen."

Rafael cocked his ear toward his companion, awaiting his thoughts.

"No," Joseph said, "I mean listen to the restaurant."

He listened. There was no conversation. He turned to see what stopped all talk. At each table, the guests were involved in eating. They did not look at each other, but gazed intently at their appetizer. And at each table, the order they devoured was *Larguini*-stuffed tomatoes.

Joseph sighed, and toyed with his fork. As if attempting to force himself to stop, but unable, he tasted one more *Larguini*. Then he gazed disgustedly about him and slammed down his fork. "I've created this monster," he said.

"It is a success," Rafael protested.

"It is ruin."

"Fantastic earnings. How can that be ruin?"

"All of these people live to eat, to fornicate, to purchase things that will give them physical pleasure. They grow fat, as I did."

"You are big with an appetite for life," Rafael said.

Joseph waved away this excuse, saying, "In the long run, all these people will not work. They will not create product, or a next generation. They will not create information, or create money because their lives will be subsumed in consuming."

Rafael found himself unable to follow Joseph's renewed vigor of thought. "As long as they buy your product, who cares how they live?"

Joseph stared at him like a man possessed of a burning idea. "Do you not see? If *Larguini* continues to grow in popularity, soon there will be no one who works. Therefore, no income to spend. No economy. No substructure holding up the price of stocks. Chaos."

Rafael tossed another forkful of the appetizer into his mouth. He saw that his guest was upset, but he could not understand the reason. He must be soothed and then talked into tackling some new project at his lab. "Joseph. Calm yourself. It cannot be as bad as all that. *Larguini* is popular, but it is not the world's only food."

His client shook his big head and leaned forward, grabbing Rafael's fork in mid-air. "Have you noticed how fast-food hamburger now is advertised as one hundred percent protein? Did you never stop to realize that phenomenal percentage cannot be accomplished with beef? Beef contains fat and protein and heaven only knows what else. How do you suppose they achieve one hundred percent protein?"

Rafael shrugged his head. He had no idea, and cared less.

"*Larguini* is one-hundred percent protein. All fast-food hamburger is now *Larguini.* It's even more addictive than salt and fat. People come back in spite of raised prices."

"So? You and I do not need to worry about that."

"And Pizza. All the meat – *Larguini.*"

Rafael tried vainly to regain control of his fork. Joseph forced him to drop the bite of stuffing. Joseph looked Rafael in the eye and said. "The whole country is eating *Larguini* at least twice a week. They can't stop themselves."

"If they can afford it, more power to them."

"We can't afford it, Rafael. The worm is insidious. If I don't return to the lab today and find an antidote to this worm, we will soon be living in a world of useless consumers. People will never again produce. Within ten years, it will be all over for you, and me, and the whole country."

"So, we export."

Joseph sat back, heavily. "God help us. Is it the spell of money, or of the worm which makes you unable to think?" Without waiting for an answer, he rose from his chair, tore the linen napkin from his vest front and threw it on the table. "Take me to the laboratory."

As if through a mist, Rafael remembered this was exactly what he'd come to talk his client into doing. Before he could comment on that fact, he noticed the shapely legs of an elegantly dressed woman who passed on her way to another table. He nearly reached out and touched the rich fur of her coat – sable, he thought it was, though he'd never paid much attention to such things.

At that moment, he noticed even Joseph's gaze followed the woman.

Joseph glanced back at Rafael. "She was mine. Last year, I think it was. I remember the coat."

Rafael tried to read either anger or jealousy in Joseph's expression, but neither was to be found on his determined countenance. Puzzled, Rafael thought he should return their conversation to its earlier, more productive trail, but he wasn't certain why.

"I must go to the laboratory," Joseph said. "Now."

Reluctantly, Rafael gathered his driving gloves. Joseph buttoned up his cashmere coat and then dropped two one hundred dollar bills on the table and led the way to Rafael's car. Once in the automobile, they talked but little, save when they passed a shop that Joseph mentioned as carrying particularly fine art objects for the home.

After dropping his friend at the lab on Wacker Drive, Rafael made an unprecedented and totally out-of-the-way side trip to Manifesto, purveyor of fine furnishings on N. Wells Street. He spent the next several hours happily ensconced in a leather chair while the consulting decorators encouraged his purchase of several *outré* pieces for the home of the discerning gentleman. As evening drew on, he reluctantly left the beautiful lamps, vases and carpets of Manifesto behind him.

He paid his bill, drew on his gloves, entered his automobile and began the drive to his office. He was certain there was much to do there, though he could not remember exactly what it might be. Driving down Michigan Avenue, Rafael Bunuel lifted one hand in a lackadaisical salute toward his office door. Instead of stopping, he returned to his condominium. He told himself that he had been working too hard for too long. All he really needed was sleep.

For the next seventy-two hours he slumbered, rousing himself only long enough to eat. He ordered in stuffed, baked tomatoes from Valdosti's.

By the time he awoke fully, he decided he'd been a fool to believe life could be only law, money making and the control of property. Life outside of his office had many sensuous experiences to offer. Rafael Bunuel determined that he would taste of each of them. He returned to his office long enough to create three partners from among the juniors in his firm. His provisions for their partnership ensured that they would carry on his work with a minimum of supervision and a maximum of income to himself. Noting the gleam of excitement in each face, he had a momentary longing to join them in the moneyed game. But the feeling lasted only through the first few sentences of a discussion of methods for the division of labor. After leaving them to sort out details, Rafael celebrated his liberation from long nights, tense meetings and the occasional unhappy client. He had grown beyond all that.

*   *

At Deny Laboratories, Joseph Bruback first tried to enlist the help of his three colleagues. He discovered them together in the common room, finishing a feast of *Larguini* Pizza. As he noted their burgeoning belts, he realized they were in no better shape than he to solve the problem. He tried to convince them of the importance of discovering an antidote to the addictive and neutering effects of the worm, but they argued that they had just discovered a real appetite for life. His worm, they claimed had shown them the need to be well-rounded by educating all the senses. They had only just begun to delve into the refinements of bodily gratification.

Joseph recognized their state. His own hand trembled as he waved away their offer of a slice of pizza. Stumbling up the steps to his laboratory, he shut and locked the door. To keep himself inside and away from temptation, he pulled his desk and several chairs in front of the closed exit.

During the next two days, he worked ceaselessly. Several generations into his worm regression, his effort to reverse the genetic make-up of his larvae still hovered beyond his ability. The problem, as he saw it was that he must re-develop the worm to become a blue and teal moth. He tried again and again to remember what he had done so that it could be undone, but his notes were hard to read, and his mind continuously wandered toward chocolate sauce.

His plan was to recreate a cocoon-making larva and then take it back to its moth stage. He needed to redevelop the moth that laid eggs and generated new worms. If he succeeded, he hoped to find a way to arrest its moth metamorphosis so that the larval stage might still look like *Larguini* while they were shipped, cooked and eaten. They must be as tasty as his original worm.

However, they must have none of the debilitating quality of that first product. Ingesting the new larva must encourage metamorphosis in those who ate them. His consumers, he believed, would then outgrow the consuming stage and return to productive life.

For forty-eight hours, he worked feverishly, in a sweat to stop the juggernaut he had created. At last, drained of ideas and of any ability to concentrate, he pulled his chairs into two facing rows and lay down to sleep. Four hours later, he awoke with a hunger unlike any he had known. He cell-phoned out for a tuna-fish sandwich. Tuna fish, he reasoned, was still free of *Larguini*. With energy sagging and his mind hovering over an image of stuffed tomato, he worked to move his desk from the opening so that the safe sandwich could be delivered.

One of his colleagues, hearing the furniture-moving commotion, knocked on his door. Through his fog of hunger, Joseph thought the man was the delivery boy. "Wait a moment," he called out. "I will get this desk moved."

"Joseph," the man said, his voice retreating, "I didn't mean to bother you."

Desperately, Joseph whispered through the door, "Please, don't go away. I need to eat."

"Ah! I have just the thing. I'll be right back."

A Boy Scout Project

Justine Pender cringed but she tried to be very quiet. She sat on the top step listening to Mom and Daddy. They were leaving. Last minute instructions to her big brother always included embarrassing stuff. They were downstairs, in the living room near the front door. They couldn't see Justine up here, but she could hear them easily.

"Rusty, be sure to turn the oven off after you make the cheese sandwiches," Mother said.

Mother was remembering the butter-melting disaster. Justine hunched her shoulders close to her ears, embarrassed. Still, she wanted to hear what else they might say.

"And don't let anyone come into the house." Daddy added. He was thinking of her encyclopedia salesman.

It wasn't her fault if things went wrong. Why did Mother and Daddy always remember her mistakes?

Whenever they left, Rusty, who was fourteen, became the babysitter. Justine was already nine years old. She didn't need a babysitter. Little brother William sure did. He got into things like the candy dish and the sawdust bin.

Thank goodness William was already asleep.

Right after the front door closed, Rusty, started to climb the stairs. Justine hurried back into her room, sat on her pink chenille bedspread, and picked up her book. She liked the adventures of

Caddie Woodlawn. She wished she had that encyclopedia too, but Daddy had called and canceled her order.

Staring at her book, she worked to read. It was hard to concentrate when Rusty's long sneaker-shoes smacked the stairs, coming closer.

Finally, he stood there, leaning on her door frame. His waves of red hair flopped over his green eyes. His freckles shone in the hall light. He smiled. His smile was nice. He didn't use it very often. He probably wanted to borrow her allowance.

"Wanta help me make something?" he asked.

"How much do you need?"

He looked puzzled. Then he laughed. "I don't need your money. I need your muscles."

That surprised her. "My spaghetti arm?" she taunted. This very afternoon he said she couldn't pitch a baseball because her arms were made of noodles.

"Hey," he said. "You pitched good." He talked that way since he started high school.

"I pitched well," she said. "And I struck out your friend."

"That's how I know you have muscles. Can you help me?"

Justine dropped her book on the bed and got up. She hitched her Levis and stuffed her feet into her penny loafers. "What are you making?"

You'll see," he said, waving at her to follow him.

They started down the stairs. Rusty walked, but Justine leaned her hands on both banisters. She let her legs swing down three steps. Then she leaned farther down the banisters, grabbed hold and swung down three more steps. As her feet swung through the air, one of her penny loafers fell off. It flew over Rusty's shoulder and landed with a thud at the bottom of the stairwell, right in front of him.

He glowered at her. "You want to wake Mr. Stinky Pants?"

"William stopped wearing diapers a zillion years ago," she said. William was in first grade.

Rusty snorted and tromped on down the stairs.

Justine said, "When you are old men, playing horseshoes in the park, I bet you'll still call him "Mr. Stinky Pants."

Rusty said, "By the time William is old, no one will play horseshoes."

She snorted at that. "Daddy says his great grandfather played it. Some games are forever."

"I'll be playing basketball," he said over his shoulder. "And Stinky will be too short to play anything."

She laughed. "Most of the old guys at the park couldn't throw a sock into a basketball hoop," she said.

Rusty didn't answer her.

"What are you building?" she asked, picking up her loafer on the way to the basement steps.

"It's a Boy Scout project." He jumped the five steps from the main floor to the basement landing. The landing shuddered.

"Who's waking William now?" she asked.

Rusty didn't answer again. He always ignored her when she was right. He turned the corner and jumped down the last five steps into the basement. He always jumped these steps, but she never could. That landing was scary. The wood squashed like a damp sponge.

She trod lightly across the mushy stair landing. Then she jumped to the concrete basement floor. She stuck close to Rusty as he started back toward Daddy's work bench. There was one light bulb working in the whole front of the basement and one back in the workbench room. She didn't want to get too far from Rusty down here in the dark.

Off to the left of the steps stood a huge cylinder of metal. That was the furnace. Around the edges of its low, wide door, she saw a flickering fire barely burning inside.

"Furnace needs revving up," Rusty said. "We'll get cold if I don't fill it."

Near the furnace, Rusty grabbed a big metal bucket called a hopper. He swung its big dark shape next to his leg as he trudged behind the furnace to the sawdust pile.

Justine stood very still. She didn't want to follow Rusty back there. There were bugs and mice in the sawdust pile. But right here, she could hear the furnace wheezing for air. Above her head, she heard air rush through the big round pipe that took heat to the living room. Nearby was another pipe that crossed the ceiling. The smaller pipe turned up through the floor. Above that place was the dining room.

All these pipes made funny crackling sounds. Daddy had explained to her that the pipes were expanding as they became warm, but the sound still made her jump. She was sure the pipes groaned.

She heard Rusty scrape a shovel full of sawdust into the hopper. Her shoulders tightened up as he put in a second shovel full. She tried hard not to shake, but she didn't like this basement. And she knew what he was going to ask her to do next.

He came back. "Open that door," he said.

She backed up from him toward the steps. "It'll burn me."

He frowned, his annoyed look. "The door is insulated. It doesn't get hot."

"Not the door. The fire inside will come out."

"Justine! What will it come out for?"

"It doesn't like being caught in there. It wants out."

He slumped, then he put the bucket down and sat on the steps. "Come here, kiddo," he said.

She stepped closer to the steps.

"Sit down beside me." He patted the stair he was on.

She sat.

"Fire isn't a being that thinks and feels," he said. "It is . . .It is an energy that you can control. Our fire heats our house."

"But I heard that a house burned down near the river last week."

"That was because the people in that house didn't control their fire. They had things that would burn sitting right up against the furnace. We won't do that."

"I don't want to open the door."

He shrugged, "Okay. Watch me do it."

She was sure he would get hurt. "Don't, Rusty."

"Justine, I do this every evening. Mom does it when we're at school. Dad does it every morning. We don't get hurt because we're careful."

She plucked at his shirt sleeve. "You need gloves to touch it?" she asked.

"No, the handle is made of Bake-Lite. It's a new material that doesn't get hot." He stood up and walked to the furnace door. Justine stood up, ready to push him out of the way of the fire. He bent over and pulled up on the door handle.

It made a squalling, metal-rubbing noise and came open.

A wave of heat rolled over her. Until that moment, she hadn't realized she was cold. There inside the metal furnace was a concrete box. Inside that box, the fire burned. It seemed dark around the edges. In the middle, it glowed orange and white. The fire didn't reach out, yet. But she didn't trust it.

"Bring me the hopper," he said, holding the door wide.

She didn't take her eyes off the fire, except to find the handle of the hopper bucket. When she lifted it, she found it was very heavy.

She carried it in front of her with both hands. It banged against her knees as she stumbled forward. She nearly fell over the hopper, but Rusty put out his hand to catch her shoulder. He shook his head as he grabbed the bucket from her.

"Watch," he said. He up-ended the bucket, pouring the sawdust into the firebox. Then he reached on the wall beside the furnace and took down a long metal-handled shovel from a nail. He used the shovel to push the sawdust pile into the glowing goals.

Flames rose from the pile. Justine pulled Rusty's arm back so the flames wouldn't follow the shovel out onto his clothes. He dropped the shovel inside the firebox.

"Hot damn!" he shouted. "What'd you do that for?"

"I don't want you to burn," she cried.

"Look at that." He pointed at the fire billowing up in the box. "Now I have to get that shovel out of there."

Justine stared at the fire and the flat end of the shovel, lying in the orange and yellow bottom of the fire. Rusty leaned toward the fire, reaching out his arm, but Justine ran forward and slammed the door shut.

"No," she turned to face Rusty. "You have to get daddy's tool."

He stood, arms hanging wide away from his body. "What tool?"

She raised her own arms, gesturing the opening and closing of the tool she remembered. "It does this," she said. "It can grab things and hangs onto them."

"What are you talking about?"

"I don't know its name. It's all crooked. It has gripper teeth, and it does this." She gestured the opening and closing again, as if she were using huge scissors.

"Get out of my way. I've got to get that thing out."

"No," she shouted, edging in front of the door. Behind her, she could feel the heat of the blazing fire inside the furnace. "Get the gripper thing."

Rusty frowned at her. He even started to push her aside, but she scissored her arms again and again, knocking him in the shoulder with her action.

"I don't know what you call it. Daddy uses it to twist big screws."

Rusty stopped trying to move her. "Oh!" he said, and ran off to the workbench room. Soon he came back with the tool Justine remembered.

"It's a bolt wrench," he said. "Now open the door."

Justine lifted the screechy door handle. As she pulled it back, she glanced across the basement to the clothesline over by the washing machine. To her relief, a long sheet hung there next to Rusty's corduroy pants. She figured she could smother the fire with the sheet if it got onto Rusty's sleeve.

Rusty opened the bolt wrench. Slowly he pushed it into the fire, grabbed the handle of the shovel and lifted it.

The shovel dropped, twisting the bolt wrench in his hands, but he grabbed tighter to the handles and went back after the shovel.

"This is going to be hot when I bring it out, so get out of the way."

The heat from the fire felt like the sunburn she had last summer. Justine stepped away. She could see that part of the shovel's flat end glowed red. She had a good idea. Grabbing the hopper bucket, she ran to the clothes-washing sink. She filled part of the bucket with water and tried to lift it out of the sink. Glancing back toward Rusty, she saw that he had dropped the shovel once more. He wiped sweat from his face.

She lifted the hopper, but it was too heavy to get all the way out of the sink. She had to pour a lot of the water back down the drain. Then, she could lift it. By the time she turned around, Rusty had the shovel part way out of the furnace door.

She tried to hold the bucket up, but it was still too heavy. It thudded to the basement floor, sloshing water all over her shoes. She couldn't lift it to carry it, so she dragged it. The bucket bottom squawked and complained with each yank, but she arrived at the furnace about the time Rusty dropped the glowing shovel on the ground.

"Don't touch it," he said. They both watched as the flat end of the shovel lit up the darkness.

"That's pretty," Justine said.

"Pretty?" Rusty said. "Now we've got to make sure it doesn't catch any dust on fire."

Justine reached into her hopper bucket with cupped hands. She scooped out water and tossed it on the shovel. Hissing steam rose. Rusty laughed. He reached down and scooped more. This time the hiss was not as deep voiced or as long. Justine scooped and tossed. They took turns until the shovel stopped making noise. It no longer glowed red.

Rusty scooped and tossed water at Justine. She sloshed him.

"That feels good." He splashed more on his face and his shirt front.

"I didn't mean to make you drop the shovel," she said.

"You shouldn't be such a scaredy cat," he said, tossing water on her blouse and face. Some of his water landed on the shovel, but it didn't steam any more.

"What were you going to build?"

"You know," he said, "I think I've done enough boy scout stuff for tonight. Mom and Dad will be home from church choir practice soon, and you're as dirty as a pig in a wallow."

"Am not."

"Go look in the mirror."

"You're a mess too," she said.

Let's build on another day."

"Build what?"

"You'll find out. But next time just open the door to the furnace for me, will you?

"You never made me any cheese sandwiches."

"I'll do that while you wash and change your shirt."

"Blouse," she said.

A Message On Linen

Translated from the original Podagrarian Language
By S.R. Williams

We have landed.

I take this ebb-tide moment to scratch our history onto the flat- surfaced fabrication which is our inheritance. Our courageous companions, the blue-flowered flax, did not survive the first few weeks at sea. Dying, the last of their members encouraged us to use all their bodies for communication with the mother colony—she even described to us how to manufacture this writing material from her stem.

We who survived thus far, fold our cotyledons together in thanks to her courage, and in hope that we have at last arrived at a hospitable shore. I will send this missive to you with our trusty bark when it leaves on the next pull of the current.

Our new latitude is north of our hoped-for destination by three mast lengths of sun-shadow. The hot disk rides low in the southern sky even though this season, by our calculations, is Warming Time. Thus, those at the upper surfaces of our vessel must hug their extensions into their central bodies in order to reduce the loss of heat. Those of us below must provide warmth to the lower extremities of those above.

Soon after the waves pushed our bark ashore, our first scout sent out a tendril, but found only small grains of quartz at our first landing zone. He has retracted onto the vessel, and we await a flood tide, hoping for better soil in which to create a home.

Long exposure to salt air has burned the most exposed parts of our bodies, but during exploration, we have discovered that it is possible to live by consuming ocean spray. Our systems seem able to filter out most of the salt, depositing it as a rime of white all about the edges of our bark. Long ago, we consumed the last food of our native soil, and for many weeks have subsisted on whatever nutrients are to be found in the air.

Some among us speculate that it is the detritus of sea kelp and other primitive oceanic life which we absorb as foodstuffs dropped upon us by the spray.

Others claim that it is the deceased bodies of our compatriots, the flax, and those of our own species whom old age has caused to decay beneath us. These, they say, are providing us the stuff of life. Whatever the cause, we are alive, and though cold and panting for fresh water, we are also in fair health. For this we are grateful.

Our bark remains remarkably buoyant, even after several seasons of following the current to this colder clime. It is our hope that the vessel will return to your shores, and that you will receive this message of hope. Please understand that with courage and a stout grip, you, our fellow di-cots, also might save yourselves from the toxins that have invaded our homeland.

*　*

One set of lighted hours have passed since last I wrote. I scratch this by the reflected light of the pocked white disk. Everyone among us longs for fresh nutrients and a solid footing. So close to good land, we are. Yet it remains far from our grasp. We know there is useful soil just beyond our reach as from here we can see enormous plant life.

On the high ground above the quartz-covered shore we note ominous, almost black, thin-leaved plants with thick brown stems appearing to be of an extremely rough texture. The leaves of these growths are so narrow that it is difficult to understand how they might enjoy enough inter-action with the light to maintain life.

The wise among us point out that what these plants lack in leaf-breadth, they make up for in leaf-abundance and thus feed themselves adequately. More than adequately, it seems; they feed to monstrous size.

The breeze brings us a pungent odor from these sturdy growths. It is not the expected savory of lighter green life, but a strong, almost intoxicatingly thick odor. And these huge plants live so closely together that, for lack of sun, few other species attempt to live beneath them.

Only one type of vine grows in their darkness. It uses every available tool to climb upward. Each vine's stem is of extraordinary thickness. Thus, the vine hoists itself upward, and is able to remain upright for long, unsupported reaches merely because of its astounding strength of stem. In several instances, two such vines can be seen twisted about each other for additional support, making a mutual effort to rise.

The vine also relies on knife-like protrusions, evenly spaced along its growing length. These protrusions help the vine cling to the thick, brown sheath of its dark host. Using these devices, the vine rises above the dark-leaved plant and reaches for light.

We are well aware that within this thicket, we will find no welcome.

*   *

Within minutes of scratching my previous sentence, the flood tide has thrown our bark upward into a high bank. In the last moments of this wild ride, we lost three of our fellow travelers – ripped from our deck and thrown out to sea. We have been watching for their bodies, but have little hope of their rescue.

We have been tossed much farther inland than I could have imagined and are thrust into a most promising soil. My fellows are now disembarking, so I cease writing and must leave this papyrus on our vessel. I hope to make my new home close enough to our ship so that I may attach more information before the next flood tide rips our boat from us and it begins the long circuit back toward you.

*   *

Our bark has settled into the high ground, so those of us not yet footed in soil must push it out to sea and risk drowning in order to send it home to you. We have devised a pole of suitable length so that only the farthest out among us are in most danger.

I have drawn the small pebble, and thus will be out on the less promising soil when our poling work is over. My fellows promise to pull me back to good soil. This will work well, but only if this green pole does not bend or break before our bark is on the tide.

I include this last-minute note to tell you that those of us dropped into soil near the giant plants of this land have already begun to thrive. New shoots may be seen on a few, and less wilting on older cotyledons. We have hope of establishing a new colony here. If this comes to fruition, we will have found a truly welcoming space.

I drop this flaxen note into the lower reaches of the bark now, and must roll to my place at the farthest end of the green pole. We, who are about to thrive, salute you.

Report of first wave, Scouts for Colonial Exploration,
Aegopodium podagraria
Signed by Colony Scribe, Gout Weed

New Life

Grace Williams discovered her new baby's knowing soul within twelve hours of giving birth to Suzannah Arwain. On that day in April 1946, barely ten months after the end of the war in the Pacific, the maternity ward at Saint Joseph Mercy Hospital in Ann Arbor, Michigan grew crowded. The staff encouraged mothers to try nursing soon after birth. They hoped in this way to reduce the bawling in the infant ward to a roaring thirty newborns at any given time.

Thus, at close on five in the evening of the baby's first day, a tight-lipped nurse brought Grace's new infant to her. She plopped the bundle of pink blanket and cellophane-taped bow into her arms and said, "You know how. You've already got three of these." Then the woman whipped the gray privacy curtains between Grace's bed and her neighbor's and marched toward the door. To Grace's astonishment, her infant actually watched the nurse stalk away. In fact, little Suzannah's scornful gaze followed the woman clear across the room.

Having had three other children, Grace was fully aware that babies of a few hours in age don't act in this manner. They don't see across rooms. They don't scorn. And most of all, they don't wait to eat.

Generally.

But in this child's case, eating waited while the baby held her breath and glared at the back of a stiff and bitter woman. When the door finally closed, Suzannah sighed, and turned her face toward Grace. Suzannah's eyes brightened. She smiled.

Grace knew better than to even think about mentioning this small sign of Suzannah's true character to anyone, including her husband, Jerry. Doctors, nurses and husbands have a tendency to explain all infant cleverness as the effect of intestinal gas.

At that moment, Jerry Williams warmed a chair in the waiting room, studying for his university finals. He was still recovering his health after years in a prisoner of war camp. He barely had enough energy to keep up work on his master's degree. He didn't need to be puzzling over a child who wasn't exactly a child.

Suzannah was different, but others would have to discover it themselves, if, and when Suzannah wanted them to know. For the moment, Grace hoped to earn the trust the baby bestowed by revealing her subtle soul to her mother.

Suzannah looked like a baby, very like her brothers and sister, in fact. Grace wondered over the infant's very large ears – not misshapen or ugly, but much bigger ears than any of her other children had at birth. She thought over each member of the family. Most of their small Michigan hometown, Williamston, had consisted of Jerry's relatives, the Williams clan, her family, the Llewellyns, with assorted Smiths and Joneses. She'd lived next door to her own Llewellyn cousins, Hugh and Davy. No big ears there. In fact, she didn't recall ears like Suzannah's in either the Llewellyn or Williams clans.

Grace fingered the circumference of one ear and whispered, "You will hear everything, the said and the unsaid."

The baby blinked, slowly. Grace cradled her infant's head in one hand, and with the other, held her bottom against mom's tummy. She carried on a soft conversation with her daughter. The discussion was one-sided, of course – even sagacious souls do not talk earlier than ordinary infants.

"Suzannah Arwain," Grace said as she pulled her gown open for the baby's mouth. "You don't like grumpy nurse Olive any more than I do, is that right?"

The baby's face pinched up. She moved her head in her mother's hand, turned it toward the door. "Don't fret," Grace soothed. "She's still gone. You want to eat?"

Solemn Suzannah returned her gaze to her mother for several seconds, then pushed her mouth toward the nearest breast and set to work. Grace crooned a silly lullaby. She had never learned proper lullabies because she constantly made up new ones to fit the baby she held in her arms.

The next child older than baby Suzannah was Ruthy. Ruthy had been born after Jerry's last leave. Ruthy was a quiet infant. In response, Grace created joyful lullabies for her.

However, soon after Ruthy's third month, Jerry's whole group was captured and force-marched up the Bataan Peninsula. They were all members of her uncle, Colonel Scott Llewellyn's division.

Early in the war, most of the boys in her Michigan town had joined up together, been assigned together to the same platoon, and many had died together in the camp on Luzon Island in the Philippines. Cousin Davy never returned. His brother, Hugh, barely survived. Jerry still showed the effects of starvation. Uncle Scott, younger brother to Grace's mother, had died there with his men.

During those years, grief, and fear for Jerry held sway. It had been a long time since Grace felt like singing at all, yet for this baby, new words came readily.

"Our Suzannah came to town
In our home she looked around,
Thought she'd try mom's lactose drink,
So her diapers rarely stink."

The baby let go of the source and pushed on the breast to raise her head an inch. She took a long, thoughtful look at the perpetrator of the song. Grace smiled at her and began a second verse.

"Our Suzannah grew up tall,

Learned roll over, and the crawl . . ."

The tune hung in the air as she mulled over rhyme options that popped into her head. She didn't like 'squall'. For seven years, life had been a fearful storm. The other rhyme that came to her mind was 'pall'. No good.

Miraculously, Suzannah held her head up, awaiting her mother's choice. Grace hurried to give satisfaction.

"Learned to sing, although she's small,

Learned we love her, one and all."

The baby rested against Grace's arm, her lips tweaked up – a gentle smile. This baby's eyes were not the usual vague blue, but dark green with amber flecks.

Back at work on the breast, Suzannah acted like any hungry baby. Grace settled down to enjoy nursing's relief from tautness. Yet, three minutes later, the baby pulled away from the nipple. Grace's breast popped from her mouth with a loud smack. It bobbed in the air between the two of them. The baby laughed.

Grace asked, "Was it stomach gas that made you laugh?"

The baby's tiny hand reached out. She pushed at Grace's breast, recreating the bobbing motion. She glanced up at her mother and laughed again. And pushed again.

Surprised, Grace laughed too. "Well, I can see you have a finely developed humor," Grace said, "but I need to get rid of some milk. Could we try the other side?"

The baby grunted. Grace put her to the other breast.

She stared down at her phenomenon, knowing they were not going to be giving this child a nickname – no Suzie, no Anna, none of that. This child would allow no diminutive. She was truly a Suzannah, a wonder. With care, she would also grow into her middle name, Arwain – the one who leads. Grace tried not to think about the other meaning of her Llewellyn grandmother's Welsh name. Arwain as a verb meant 'to carry the burdens of others'.

Three months passed. During that time, Grace learned that Suzannah's small, but ancient soul created as much fun and as much trouble as her older children. Still, an occasional questioning look from Suzannah, or a sudden turn of her daughter's head would make Grace wonder aloud about what Suzannah knew. She spoke to the baby as if to a friend. The baby listened. With her large ears, she seemed to hear everything and understand more.

Jerry, who studied astronomy called them "Star-finder ears" after a new bowl-shaped astronomical antenna he'd read about. One evening, he pretended to be a star beeping a Morse Code message toward Suzannah's ears. The baby giggled and reached for her father's face. In a sudden motion, he pulled back and stared at her.

"You . . ."

"What is it, honey?" Grace asked.

Jerry glanced at her, his face dark with what she had come to know as Memory – the terror and exhaustion of the march, the despair of the prisoner-of-war camp, the death of friends about whom he would never speak.

"No," he said to the baby, ignoring Grace's question. "It's just your daddy's crazy mind acting up. You're my innocent Baby Snooks, Suzannah Arwain, my sweet one."

Grace thought about such moments, but knew she could not get Jerry to tell her what they meant. She believed Jerry studied the stars in order to escape the earth. He knew too much about life on earth. At home, he wanted their life to be separate from the ugliness he'd known, separate and clean.

So, she made up lullabies, built Lincoln Log villages with the children, and read Golden Books to all. With Jerry, she offered solace and love when he could accept them.

Suzannah was three months old on July fourth weekend, a four-day vacation from Jerry's university studies. The whole family left Ann Arbor to camp along the Huron River. They planned to meet Jerry's surviving army buddy, cousin Hugh on Friday. On Sunday, they planned to drive to Grandma Llewellyn's.

Before Hugh arrived, Grace's family took a short hike along the river. Suzannah rode in a back-pack Jerry had rigged up. From her perch on Jerry's back, Suzannah could see everything in front of Jerry as well as on all sides of the trail.

She rode silently, rocking and studying, keeping an eye on her family as if she were responsible for any stragglers on the march. When her brother, Jon, disappeared around the next bend, she cried and pointed. Then, when they all turned the corner and he reappeared, Suzannah relaxed.

Grace noticed Suzannah didn't take her eyes off Jon again for several minutes. He continued to stay in sight, so the baby began to make brief glances about her at the trees and the sunshine.

"Dott," she said, suddenly. Then more loudly, "Dott! Dott!" And her stout arm flung out to the side of the pack.

The other children gathered about her. "Her first word is Dad," shouted Daniel.

Jerry glanced over his shoulder. "It's way early to be talking. Besides, she's not pointing at me."

"I bet she's pointing at some dog," Jon said.

But Suzannah pointed more firmly toward the river.

Little Ruthy studied the line of Suzannah's gaze. "She's looking at the ducks. She's saying 'Duck'."

Suzannah shouted. Three mallards, startled by her squeals, took off, flapping across the wide river. As they rose, she pointed up and up. The rest of the day, she crowed about 'Dotts', as if the sound might do all further communicating.

When they arrived, Cousin Hugh had barely exited his Studebaker before he took a good look at the baby and said, "Where'd the big ears come from?"

"She'll grow into them," soothed his wife, Judy.

Suzannah pointed at Hugh and sang out, "Sdott. Sdott."

Jerry chuckled. "She's calling you a duck, big guy."

Hugh and Jerry unloaded and put up two large camping tents. At their tent, Jerry zipped the mosquito screening, but tossed the heavy canvas door-flap back over the roof of the tent and out of the way.

"There," he said. "Now you kids be sure to keep the netting zipped. Don't want flies and mosquitoes sleeping with us."

After a day of canoeing and swimming, the adults wrapped chicken, corn and butter in tinfoil to roast in the coals. Dinner tasted warm and wonderful. When the dishes were dry, all settled around the campfire.

The evening wind came up as they sang. Boisterous songs died down to 'Tenting Tonight'. A thoughtful mood settled over the adults, and sleepiness over the children. Suzannah let out a squeaky yawn.

Grace sighed. She didn't want to begin the whole bedtime ritual for four children. The older children still enjoyed the art of turning marshmallows into ash. Grace decided on a compromise.

"I'll take her into the tent, Jerry. You can bring the other children later."

Jerry glanced up. "In a few minutes, dear."

She lifted Suzannah and walked the fifteen yards to the tent, talking to the baby about the day. As they approached the tent, wind gusted, lifted the canvas door flap and tossed it with a whomp down over the doorway. Suzannah cringed. She grabbed Grace's sweater front.

"No!" Suzannah whimpered. "Never again."

Startled, Grace saw her daughter's mouth shape the words, heard the sounds, and saw her green eyes open wide in terror. The wind rustled the tent flap again.

The baby cried out. "Don't take me in. They'll hurt me."

Grace's body went cold. Three-month old Suzannah said words – clear, coherent sentences. Grace's heart pounded. This was no awkward baby talk, no baby thoughts. Her child's soul forced terror into words – a fear so powerful it followed her into this life.

Grace stood, stunned. The wind again whipped the tent.

Suzannah cried out, "Knives cut."

Behind them at the fire, the children sang with Jerry, Judy and Hugh. 'The Eeenstie, Beanstie Spider'.

In her arms, Suzannah sobbed. Grace turned away from the awful tent; away from the innocent children at the fire; away from her husband and her cousin who already knew too much of terror. She marched left, down a path into the woods, asking, "Who are you afraid of, Sweetheart?"

"The men. They'll take me in the tent and cut me."

"We're not going into the tent." Grace forced her voice to be firm.

"Please. Not there. Not there."

Horror made the baby deaf to assurances. Grace wanted to know more, but her mother instinct refused to ask anything from this terrified soul. She had to help the new baby believe anguish was over, the other, horrible life finished.

Suzannah's new life would be fresh and as safe as a mother could make it.

The child voice continued to plead and cry in adult words. Grace wrapped her sweatered arms around Suzannah, sheltering her from the past. She curled one hand about her head and used her pointer finger to touch the baby's cheek. In this quiet way, she got Suzannah's attention.

"Suzannah," she said firmly. "You and I will sleep in the car tonight."

Suzannah's sobbing words ceased, but she shuddered again and again. Grace spoke with authority, like one who could hold all threats at bay.

"You are now my little girl. You are with me. No other place, nor any other time. You are my baby, Daddy's baby. You are Jon's sister, Daniel's sister, Ruthy's sister. You are loved. You are safe."

Suzannah's green eyes watched Grace's mouth. Amidst a long sob, tears coursed down her cheeks. Grace added new ideas as they came to her, praying her words would let the child put away the past.

"Jon will teach you to walk and run. Daniel and you will play with trucks and cars. Ruthy will show you how to sing and dance and . . ."

Suzannah's rigid body relaxed. They walked down the path, then turned back by way of the road so they wouldn't pass the tent. At last, Suzannah dropped into a profound sleep.

Grace whispered to Jerry, "The tent frightened Suzannah. We'll spend the night in the car." He raised his eyebrows, but kissed the baby goodnight and promised to make sure the children brushed their teeth before bedtime.

During the next day, the children stayed near, so Grace couldn't explain to Jerry. Little Suzannah said nothing all day. At bedtime the second night, Suzannah allowed Ruthy to carry her into the tent to sleep in the midst of her brothers and sisters.

On Sunday, the family drove from the campground to visit Grace's Grandmother Llewellyn. After the war and rehab, Jerry had explained to Grandma that her son, Colonel Scott Llewellyn, was not missing. He'd died in the camp on Luzon Island. Jerry would not talk about how men died in that camp even though Jerry and Grandma had a special relationship because of Uncle Scott's important place in their lives.

When they arrived, Grandma offered cinnamon rolls and warm affection to her family. Toward evening, Grandma asked Grace to bring her the maple jewelry box, where she had a gift for the new baby. Grace hiked Suzannah up on her hip and walked back to the bedroom. She leaned over the dresser, searching for the old maple box.

Suzannah said, "Sdott."

Grace glanced up. Her baby's finger pointed to a photo of Grace's Uncle Scott, an old Brownie Box picture taken when he was about ten. The photo was black and white, but somehow, Grace knew the flecks in his eyes were amber on green. And there, on his young head, were the ears.

So, she thought, as a kid, he had the Star-Finder ears. By the time she remembered him, he was already an adult, a colonel. He'd grown into his ears, as Judy predicted for Suzannah.

Grace lifted the worn frame. From another lifetime, Scott's solemn eyes gazed out and his mouth turned up with a gentle smile at the camera, at Grace and Suzannah. The thickness of his jacket hinted that he'd been hunting. Behind Scott, a dark goose took off from the lake.

Baby Suzannah reached toward the glass. She pointed at the flying goose and said, "Dott."

Her finger passed over the goose to rest on Scott's cheek.

"Sdott," she said.

"Oh," Grace whispered.

Suzannah glanced up, touched her mother's tear-stained face, then placed her baby hand on her own chest, murmuring, "I Sdott."

"Yes," Grace said. "You are Sdott. And now, you are Suzannah Arwain, our pearl, a leader, the carrier of burdens."

The baby leaned her head on Grace's shoulder, her arms around her mother's neck. The next words she spoke clearly came at eighteen months, a normal time for a new child.

Apopka And The Holy Land

I've found a way to get
the Holy Land Experience
Right on Millenia Mall.
Fifteen miles north of Orlando,
Way far north of Disney world,
The Millenia Mall offers what looks
From I-5
To be the whole grand view
From Jezebel's Tower
The Home of Herod the Butcher,
The manger scene in lights
On the freeway you are
near Pilate's Judicial Court.
The whole scheme and teachings
Right here in Florida
-on sand raised out of the sea
Sometime less than six thousand years ago,
Or so the preacher said.

So tomorrow,
I'm for sure gonna stop for
The Holy Land Experience,
because this winter,

When Aunt Joan intones
The age-old prayer
"Next year in Jerusalem",
I can say,
"Been there. Done that.
Let's do next year
at Epcot Center."
That's the plan.
But today I'm by-passing
the Holy Land
for a visit
to the less biblical
though still blessed
plant nurseries
of the town of
Apopka.

A Custom Observed

Motorized Metal Tool Worship
By courier ship:
To Elder Council
from Third Planet Exploratory Mission

Our exploratory group has landed on the third planet from the star called Helios. We landed in a green space in an urban center within the (more or less) rectangular land mass which exists halfway between this planet's equator and its northern pole.

Our observations compare quite closely with those who landed in rural areas of the same land mass. The custom we are about to describe to you appears to be common to this land mass only. It is not observed in either of the triangular land masses below the central meridian to any great extent. Nor is it observed in most of the other, large land mass in the north.

This custom we have termed "Motorized Metal Tool Worship". It has been observed that whenever the sun is visible in the areas defined above, large numbers of the males among the two-legged species open their adjunct storage containers and bring out noise makers constructed of metal. Often these consist of a gas-powered motor, housed in the admired color (yellow or green are most common). To these motor housings is attached any one of a variety of wands or ritual cutting tools.

The male straps one of these apparati upon his back and walks around marking his territory by waving the wand or blade at items on the periphery of his area of control.

The motor emits a high and potentially ear shattering whine. The more intelligent among the two-legged males protects his own ears from the whine of his own green or yellow apparatus. It is believed that this noise is one of the principle powers of the motorized metal – warning other males, and even females among them, to stay well away from the male as he proceeds with his ritual.

It is more common in the urban areas for the attachment to be a wand that blows air at the periphery of the male's territory. In rural areas, the-metal-waving male more often uses a blade. This blade is one of their hands wide and anywhere from five to seven hand spans in length. It is surrounded by moving teeth which can cut through very thick vegetation. In these areas, man and vegetation are warned not to encroach upon the male with the wand.

It is believed that the use of metal wands and blades provides the male with a sense of security. It is what allows him to remain on polite terms with other males of his species. By waving wands and blades in the presence of the other, each knows the limits of his area of influence.

When the wand or blade-waving worship is finished. The male retreats to his secondary storage unit. The careful among them hang the metal apparatus on the side walls of the storage unit. Others merely drop the apparatus on the floor and return either to the primary storage unit or to the more public areas of their influence region.

Some may, after warning others with the wand, spend some time fraternizing with the neighboring males, leaning upon another apparatus that could be seen as a warning device.

This new device has no motor. It consists of a long roundish handle atop a wide metal bar that offers sharpish teeth to fend off any approach of the neighboring male. When a male is not leaning upon this device as a warning to others, the metal teeth can be used to yank up the plant material nearby. It is thought that yanking up plant material may be another way of advertising the ferocity of the male who practices this act.

This report submitted by
Gorzo, secretary of Third Planet Exploratory Mission

Note: Our next report will cover larger tools employed in what we will call Yellow Metal Worship – tools that run on large cogs and have an assortment of metal attachments.

These Yellow Metal Tools can be made to move about in all directions. They bite and spit out massive amounts of the third planet's rock and soil surface. We continue to study the purposes of using these tools and are not certain if they are also meant to advertise ferocity and warn others about property rights.

Often, they are used to prepare surfaces that can later be covered with a hot steaming substance the inhabitants call 'asphalt'. These asphalt surfaces crisscross the entire northern landmass and, when cooled sufficiently, are used to facilitate yet another interesting tool that seems to come in all colors. (a third report being developed by our observation team).

Sóspiro's Restorative

At ninety-three years and several months of age, Mr. Sóspiro needed to brace himself for the small wonder of energy he knew was coming. He flexed his arms, smiled and hummed a tune as he checked the clock on his studio wall. Three minutes until three o'clock on Monday afternoon. Seven-year-old Robby would arrive for his violin lesson at one minute before three.

From Sóspiro's experience, he knew the lesson would be a whirlwind hour, beginning with the child's habitual announcement, "Have I got a surprise for you", and ending with his closing statement, "I think I've got it good, and I need to pee."

There was not much question about who was in charge of Robby's lesson. Sóspiro wondered if the boy's Celtic dance teacher was as happy, and as worn out, after an hour with Robby.

He chuckled at the thought. Such energy. Such a mind. Such a wonder-filled child.

With two minutes before Robby's arrival, Sóspiro lifted his violin to his aching shoulder and warmed his strong, agile fingers. He knew Robby could hear this violin from the moment he bounded out of his mother's SUV. Listening to his teacher was part of the learning. There would not be many more lessons. Sóspiro wanted the boy to remember the sound of careful, vigorous practice.

He played three octave scales and arpeggios. During the augmented-seventh arpeggio, Robby cracked open the door to the studio. The boy never merely entered. He always peeked, and then dashed in.

Sóspiro acted as if he didn't see the child, but he too peeked, watching the small, pale face peer around the door jamb. The boy's blond shock of hair nearly covered his dark brown eyebrows. Beneath his straight-cut bangs, his big eyes watched his teacher's fingers and then his attention moved to the bow, finally focusing on the little finger of the bow hand.

Good, thought Sóspiro. He watches the right things.

The boy's head moved up and down, following bow strokes. At the back of his head, an ever-present cowlick bobbed stiffly.

Willful hair, thought Sóspiro as he played the upper octave and started back toward the lower. Willful hair and willful boy who wants to learn everything.

He pretended to be absorbed in playing the augmented-seventh, expecting soon to hear Robby's opening announcement, then his bursting in, and finally his dash to hug his teacher. No doubt today's surprise would be the revelation that Robby had taught himself the rest of Lully's Gavotte with which Sóspiro had whetted his appetite last Monday. He reached the bottom of the arpeggio, spun out the resonance of the lowest note and then glanced at the boy.

"Well, hello," Sóspiro said.

"I have a surprise for you."

"You learned to tie your shoes, no?"

An ear to ear grin greeted this guess. "No. . . I mean yes. I mean, I have something to show you."

"A special gavotte, perhaps." Sóspiro opened his arms, violin and bow in one hand, the other free for the running hug. For some reason, Robby hung back, hovering in the hallway.

"Uhm. I have learned the Gavotte," the child said, raising his small violin case into view, "but I've also got something else." He opened the door a little wider. Sóspiro saw that he wore an extra-large Trailblazer tee-shirt. It nearly covered his corduroy shorts. On his feet were dirty blue gym shoes and startling white socks, one pulled up to his skinned knee, the other fallen about his ankle, revealing a long bruise on his shin.

"Come in, little man," Sóspiro urged. It puzzled him that today the boy was so reticent.

Robby stepped into the room followed by an odd apparatus. Attached to his back was a hump of blue and green – a shine, and yet a softness in the color. Sóspiro pushed at his glasses, but the hump still appeared to be attached to the child. The boy reached awkwardly around its bulk to close the studio door. The color and texture that followed him began to unfurl, slowly fanning out so that Sóspiro saw the structure beneath – not a hump, but two arches of bone and two swoops of flexible cartilage softened by iridescence and shimmer.

His pulse leapt with a tremolo of fear. Wings. The boy had wings.

"In a school play, were you?" he asked, but he could see the wings were not a costume.

"Nope. Just grew them. It only took about five days." Robby remained close to the door, his violin case held across his chest like a cradled pet "I wanted to learn to fly, see, so I slept with this pigeon wing-feather I found down at Wilshire Park."

Sitting in his straight-back chair, Sóspiro tried to take a deep breath, but it caught in his throat. His left arm went limp with the numbness that had been attacking it lately. Using deliberate movements, he took the violin and bow from his left hand and laid them on the small Persian carpet he always kept on his studio table. His mind worked quickly over the enigma of the wings.

Pigeon feathers do not produce wings, he reminded himself. I am having a stroke.

After long seconds, he turned toward Robby.

The boy smiled slightly. His ears always rose when he smiled. Now, the wings rose as well, threatening to brush Sóspiro's painting of a desert canyon from the studio wall.

"Oops," said Robby, stepping toward his teacher.

"Paintings are replaceable," said Sóspiro, trying to keep his voice from betraying his deepest concern. *Dear God, don't let me die in front of this child.* "You should maybe get the violin out so we can hear today's surprise," he said with forced evenness to his tone.

"Okay." The child's glance took in the possibilities for how to move, and where to put the case without knocking down artwork.

At first, Sóspiro thought it best to ignore the mirage of the wings, and the danger. If this were not a stroke, he thought . . . but it had to be a stroke. Real wings were impossible. To maintain his calm for the boy's sake, he decided at last to pretend the wings were there, but not surprising.

"Large wings in a small space – a big problem," he said.

The boy nodded his head in a vehement motion that set his cowlick bobbing like a cock's comb.

"A huge problem," Robby agreed. "I could barely fit in the van, and Mom refused to let me fly over; I haven't had much practice landing."

"Well then," Sóspiro dragged in air, attempting rational thought. "We must find a way to fit into the studio. In order to avoid turning around, how about putting the violin case on my lap and . . . and opening it there?" He'd almost offered to open it himself, but the feeling had not yet returned to his left hand.

He wondered at his own selfishness. He should have introduced the child to a younger teacher weeks ago when this numbness first began to come on him. But he had wanted to be with Robby, wanted to see his bobbing hair and hear his incessant curiosity. Now, God forbid, it might be too late.

He glanced again at the blue iridescence – as solid as the child's sturdy legs. Such a prodigious talent in one so young was fraught with enough difficulties – never mind adding blue and green wings.

The boy plopped his instrument case on his teacher's thin-legged lap and flipped the button on the spring-operated closure. As Robby bent over his job, Sóspiro stared down. The wings moved constantly – opening, then closing back against each other. In the back of the black and red Trail Blazer's tee-shirt, there were ragged slits, no doubt made by the child's mother to accommodate the bulk of feather and bone. Through those holes, Sóspiro could see that the wings flexed from the ridge of each scapula. The muscles on either side of Robby's backbone were enlarged and red, as if enflamed.

Over-worked, Sóspiro thought. How can the boy carry all this weight?

As the feathers moved under the fluorescent light of the studio, the blue deepened to purple and back to turquoise.

Robby glanced up at his teacher, revealing a darkness in his lower eyelids that Sóspiro had not noticed before.

"I haven't practiced as much as I wanted," the child said. "I've been learning to fly, and then sleeping a lot."

"Well, let us hear your piece," Sóspiro said gently. "Later, we can discuss how to deal with this heavy responsibility."

The boy's cowlick waved with the motion of his bow as he tuned his violin in perfect fifths. Sóspiro set the violin case on the floor, grabbed at his numb hand with his good one and sat up again to watch. Robby set his feet apart, lifted his instrument, and swung his bow onto the A string. One of his wings opened toward Sóspiro. It flexed, marking two silent quarter notes before the opening of the dance. Robby pulled straight and true, producing full, ringing tones. He played with such self-confidence and energy it was easy for Sóspiro to imagine courtiers and ladies leaping and whirling across a dim, torch-lit hall to the accompaniment of a seraphic musician.

But when the last chord rang out, the child was breathing heavily. Sweat dripped from his forehead.

"You played wonderfully."

"But I can't play very long." In his distress, Robby held his precious violin in front of his face, leaning his reddened cheek against its tight-grained back for coolness.

Sóspiro took the violin and bow from him, set them on the table's Persian carpet next to his own, and then he opened his arms. The boy fell into his lap with such haste that Sóspiro had to work quickly to envelope the wings within his frail hug.

Robby's mouth pulled tight, holding back tears. He looked hopefully up at his teacher. Sóspiro weighed the import of the child's glistening eyes as he sought out what to say.

"You wanted to fly, yes?"

"I didn't know they had to be so big."

"How could you know? It is like wanting to play the violin – a little wanting, and then the thrill of the first song, and then the second – each song more beautiful and more complicated than the last, until your whole life is music."

"I wanted wings on my feet – like the god that brings flowers."

Sóspiro blinked, trying to understand. "Ah, the god Mercury." He glanced down at the boy, and whispered, like one telling a forbidden truth, "I suspect those piddly little wings of his are aerodynamically unsound."

Through his tears, Robby snickered, and then replied. "I wanted them for dancing, to make my leaps bigger."

Sóspiro leaned his head to one side, considering that idea as he stroked the feathers. "It might have worked."

"Yeah," the boy said, rousing from his despair, "Woulda been good for basketball, too."

"An unfair advantage on the court, don't you think?"

A thoughtful frown puckered the skin between Robby's eyebrows. "I guess they'd need to make new rules for flying players."

"No landing on the backboard to dunk, maybe," Sóspiro suggested. As they talked, Sóspiro brushed his hand through the long primary feathers at the finger end of the left wing. One bright blue-green feather came loose and lay in his palm. Robby seemed not to notice, but sank into his teacher's quickly tiring arm.

"These big wings make dancing hard," Robby said as Sóspiro laid the feather next to the violins and then shifted the child's weight and the wings closer to his chest. "And at school," the boy continued, "I don't fit my desk. And the sharing rug is too small for my friends and my wings to be together."

"That is not good," Sóspiro said. "But where is your magic pigeon feather?"

"It disappeared."

"Lost?"

"No. Each night that my wings were growing, the feather became smaller and smaller. It disappeared."

Sóspiro raised his eyebrows and thought a moment. "What did you do besides sleep on this feather?"

The little boy's hand rested on Sóspiro's heart as he spoke. "Before bedtime," Robby said, "I talked to the birds in our oak tree. I told them what I wanted."

"And they agreed?"

Robby shrugged. "They chirp and whistle. I can't understand them, you know."

His old teacher smiled at Robby's imaginative fantastique. After moments of silence, he felt life returning to his left hand even though he held the boy. He also recognized signs of the child's growing drowsiness. He knew he could not hold Robby's weight plus the weight of the wings for much longer, so he leaned over and touched the boy's cowlick with his lips before whispering.

"I will do some research on this question of the wings. As soon as I find an answer for how to ungrow them, I will let you know."

Robby sat up and touched Sóspiro's face. "I knew you could help."

"I will do my best for you. Now what do you say about playing one more piece before you depart?"

The boy climbed from his lap, a little of his old energy returning. "I want to do that arpeggio – the one you did when I came today."

Sóspiro smiled. Practicing the augmented-seventh arpeggio had been a calculated choice. By its nature, its notes haunted musicians, holding out a promise, but never arriving at a musical resting place.

"To do all three octaves of the arpeggio," he said, "you must learn to fly out of first position and use the whole length of your fingerboard."

"I've been watching you do that," Robby said. "I think if you show me how, I can learn it."

Sóspiro had no doubt it was true. In the twenty minutes left to them, between short stops to rest his shoulders, Robby negotiated several respectable three-octave arpeggios up and down his violin. Then he wiped his wet forehead and announced, "I think I've got it good, and now I need to pee."

Sóspiro nodded, "You have it good, indeed. And you know where the bathroom is."

Robby reached down next to his teacher's chair and began replacing his violin in its case. Sóspiro studied the feathers where they swept the floor as they opened and closed. He lay one hand on the boy's back, between the wings. Closing his eyes, he absorbed the heat from the child's tired muscles.

A moment later, Robby straightened, violin case in hand. He reached with his free arm to hug his teacher. As Sóspiro brushed his cheek against the little boy face, he knew what he must say.

"I'll see you next Monday," Robby said.

"Ah. Did I not tell your mother about my vacation?"

Robby shook his head.

"How thoughtless of me. I will be traveling for the next little while. I will call your mother with the name of a very fine teacher who will substitute for me while I am gone."

He saw Robby swallow hard, and his pinched face grow pale.

"Don't worry, I will call with information about the wings," he assured the boy, but he knew even then that the cumbersome, tiring wings were not the child's main concern. In the loss of a dear friend, only time would help.

"Now scoot out to the bathroom before Mother comes searching for you."

Robby swished his blue-green wings to the door. After he opened it, he turned, glancing around one wing to check on his teacher. Sóspiro kept up his encouraging face long enough for that expected glance. Then, when the boy was gone, his own gaze turned to his left hand, lying limp in his lap.

After he heard the toilet flush, and after the door to the parking lot opened and closed, he lifted the loosened feather from the Persian carpet table cover. Feeling the smooth texture of its quill, he knew that his left hand might work again within the hour. But he also knew there was no telling how much longer it would be able to recover from such numbing events.

He put down the feather, lifted the phone from his desk and dialed the number for an admired colleague. When his friend answered, he began the difficult sentence.

"Joseph, I have a very young student I would like you to help. He is extraordinary and he will need you soon."

By Wednesday, the hump in Sóspiro's back was palpable, and painful. When he called Robby's mother, her relief broke through her reserve as she told him that the boy's wings grew shorter each night.

They were already of a length that could be covered by his ordinary tee shirts. Robby was feeling much better.

When Sóspiro mentioned his friend, Joseph, she was at first dismayed. But with a few words, he calmed her concerns and assured her that Robby would be in the best of hands until he returned from his journey.

After he hung up, Sóspiro lay on his bed and whispered to the robin in the maple outside his open window. "I wish to fly soon. Will you teach me to fly?"

Robin called "Cheerio, cheerio," and ended his comment with a long trill.

Sóspiro reached with his good hand to make sure the blue-green feather was still beneath his pillow. The feather was small, now, and difficult to locate, but it lay there. Sóspiro closed his eyes and hummed Lully's Gavotte for Robin until they both fell asleep.

Ball's Bluff Battlefield

Woody and I are in Virginia in May. He for an opportunity to help teach ethics and public speaking skills to fellow actuaries, me for research on our nation's history.

Yesterday, after we both visited the great battlefield at Gettysburg, we were in deep sadness. So many feared, sweat, starved, and died in such bloody and mundane little fields and groves; so many were mown down in that final charge across what amounts to two football fields in corn and wheat; and so many stood firm, only to lose their lives, when others ran.

Today, while Woody teaches, I want to be by myself somewhere in Virginia where nature is the focus. On the maps, I cannot find a park, arboretum or even a rose garden that is within visiting distance for the time that I have. But I do find a small memorial battlefield about twenty miles from our hotel. On the map, I notice a stream running next to the park, and what appear to be the close lines indicating a bluff on the battlefield side of the map. Across the stream, farmland. Maybe a small battlefield surrounded by river and farmland will lift this cloud from my soul.

So, I bid goodbye to Woody. I climb into our rented car, and with the aid of a GPS sporting an incongruously bubbly voice, I drive past shopping malls toward the north. The day is bright. The air warms. The sun on the wet pines makes iridescent sparkles. Virginia is in its rainy season, but today is beautiful.

I pass the sign to the battlefield along the way, realize my mistake and drive another five miles before I find a mall in which I can turn around. Returning south, I slow and signal the left turn. Almost immediately on my entrance into the park, I find I am in a completely empty parking lot. No other historic site we've visited has been this devoid of human activity, or lacking materials for sale. Here, there is nothing but the path and the signs.

I get out, lock the car and begin following what happened in this place in 1861.

I have no familial connections to this or any other battlefield in Virginia. Both of my father's grandfathers, the Williams and the Wheeler grandfathers who engaged in war, fought in the south. They had been, and later again were neighbors, across the road from each other in a border state.

The big grandfather, Chester A. Williams, rode as a cavalry officer for the Union. The little grandfather, Albert Wheeler, was a blacksmith for the Army of the Confederacy.

The war history of my mother's Stamps and Chaplain grandfathers, in Arkansas, is less clear, but nowhere near Virginia. So, I am not searching for roots in my battlefield visit, only information in this small place, and a respite from other knowledge as well – the knowledge of the horrific stupidity when proud generals send hundreds across an open field in the slim hope that numbers will overwhelm large-bore, well-aimed guns.

This park, called Ball's Bluff, is quiet. Though I am its sole visitor, birds welcome me with whippoorwill softness and robin chirrup. The undergrowth is natural – a Virginia forest, open spaces, a mix of southern oak varieties, of birch and pine trees – wet wildness after yesterdays' downpour. I am seeing more oak varieties than we have in Oregon. One genus can have such wildly different leaves.

I begin to follow what happened here in that fall of 1861. Reading signs that poke above the underbrush, I soon leave the sad whippoorwill behind me. I see where Confederates camped to rest over there on the meadow land. I imagine the night, the tents, the campfires kept low because the soldiers know that the Union has troops across the stream in the farmland.

Here, Confederates are within thirty miles of Washington D.C. and in the no-man's land contested by both armies.

Several times during this war, the Army of the Confederate States has threatened the Union capital. This small contingent is poking in that direction again, perhaps the vanguard, or maybe the rearguard of a larger force. Only these sixteen hundred Confederates lie between the Union troops and possible capture of Leesburg by the U.S. Army of Northern Virginia.

Leesburg is to the west. However, to the east, between Union and Confederate troops lies the Potomac River and a very steep bluff, about fifty feet of difficult climb up from the river. Confederate guards on this side, and across the river, Union guards, watch the riverbank for any activity.

The robin who first greeted me follows, hopping from branch to branch as I approach the bluff and the depression in which the Confederate watch made themselves safe from snipers of the other persuasion. The energy of the robin's chirruping belies the memory of what happened on this side of the Potomac.

During that time, in the night, downstream and around a bend, the Union leaders sent a reconnaissance of a few boats and several dozen troops. The bluff is less steep around the bend, the waters, slower. The scouts discerned an opportunity and sent back for more troops.

The attack on the Confederate camp came through here, from the northeast, taking the few watchmen by surprise and catching the main Confederate group in their tents. But soon the guards along the stream rallied and gave the others a chance to arm and get into action.

Here died a Union leader and U.S. Senator, Edward Baker, there a Confederate guard. Over there, several Union men lay in the underbrush, raking the camp with rifle fire before the Confederates were able to escape and regroup.

The camped Confederates were outnumbered by the Union, and surprise had almost won in the initial moments. I walk down into the hollow where the Union mass entered the area. I'm followed by the robin who seems more curious than angry at my intrusion.

I see where, in the dark, the Union soldiers could not tell they were on the low ground in a long path worn into the land by the occasional overflow creek of flood times. While I am here, I can see that yesterday's rain has left this hollow a soggy waterway.

During that night of invasion, when the Confederates escaped the light of their own fires and the strafing fire of the invaders, they regrouped on the high ground above this small depression. Confederates were a mere seven feet higher than the Union men, but enough to have the advantage. Plus, they had camped here for three days, and so knew the hollow and the soggy ground that caught at boots and slowed attack or escape.

The surprise by the Union lasted maybe twenty minutes, and then, the greater knowledge of the land resulted in death, here in the bog, over there in the copse of trees. Union troops escape back to the Potomac River meant tumbling down the bluff, or stumbling north, retreating to the boats still moored around the bend.

Behind that boulder, lay a Confederate sharpshooter. Death to the man who had shiny metal upon him in the dark. Within four hours, the remnant of the Union sortie had stumbled back to the boats or was lost or captured in that general direction.

But a Union contingent of seven hundred out of the three thousand original group, had scrambled down or fallen to the narrow land, the crumbling riverbank at the bottom of the bluff. They held out down there, hiding behind rocks and scraggly trees, but their remnant spent the rest of the war in the same prisoner of war camp as my Williams great-grandfather – Andersonville.

I follow the men running north, and then turn back to learn more about what happened to the Union troops in the bluff area. Almost a thousand Union men died in this route, and around one hundred fifty Confederate soldiers.

As I approach the top of the bluff again, the sound of the bird stops suddenly. The robin which has accompanied me in my wanderings through this underbrush flashes away with a rush of fear. Her wings thump the air and then stop.

I feel a change that I can't identify – a cold moment on my neck, a tightening of my scalp. I know I must get out of here, though why, I cannot explain to myself. And I am about a half mile from my car.

I run, nearly tripping on tree roots, avoiding the low-land bog which makes my escape a ragged zigzag. I don't look back, I just flat out run. I pass the markers of Union and Confederate death. I pass the birches, the boulders, the pine trees. I smack through oak leaves and race to my car, keys in hand, beeping the driver's door.

I slam inside, pulling the door after me and locking it. I start the motor and at that moment, lightning strikes the parking lot twenty feet away, between where I am and where I was. Clouds roar into the Potomac Valley, covering the sun. Rain sheets down.

After a sweating fear-filled minute, I back out of my lonely space, head for the entrance and glance behind me at another flash of lightning.

Twenty minutes later, I have followed the brake lights of a line of cars, the only thing one can see in the heavy waves of rain. At last, I am parked in the hotel lot. The rain and wind continue to whip the trees, but the lightning seems to be behind me, back in the direction of the battlefield and the shopping malls. I decide to brave the rain, and race from car to hotel. Once inside, I text my husband, who is teaching. "I am in the hotel and safe."

Woody texts back, "Tornado winds expected, we've been moved away from windows and into the interior bar. Come down to level B."

"Level B."

Such a modern phrase to wrench me from the past to the present.

The Palmse Music Box

August 20, 1991

In the early morning of August 20th, 1991, thirty-year old Mikhel Aivar Krichevsky stood with one hundred friends from nearby towns and farms of Estonia. They faced across the narrow source of the Narva River, blocking the way to the Jõhvi-Vasknarva Road. On the far side, sat five Russian tanks.

From this location, Mikhel could look down river where other tanks lined the river on the eastern side, and Estonian people stood together on the west. He knew that at every narrow between Lake Peipsi and Lake Lämmi his people sang toward the silent and frightening tanks.

The people held hands. The tanks pointed their guns toward the sky.

"All's quiet on the western front," quipped Mikhel.

"For the time being," Anja Saarela said. "But let us sing."

Mikhel glanced at her, the dark-haired girl he had known all his life, the girl he loved, though she never seemed aware of that fact. He had long ago admitted that Anja truly led here, though he was the one who waved his arms. Anja became the force at the Narva – dedicated, courageous and shining. Anja truly loved this land of trees, lakes and bogs. She loved the possibility of living in a land once again free from invaders.

Anja whispered "Eesti and then Russ."

Sing in Estonian and then in Russian.

So, Mikhel moved in front of the local group. He raised his arms and said, "*Mu Isamaa.*"

Everyone understood his reference. When he brought down his arms on beat one, all sang the poem of Lydia Koidula to the music of Gustav Ernesaks.

"My fatherland is my love."

As he conducted, he heard other groups of Eesti down river begin to join *Mu Isamaa.*

He had no doubt that across the river, the men of the Soviet tanks loved their mountains, the plains and even the swamps of their land as well. When he had served in the Soviet army, he had heard them sing, talk and tell stories about their families, their farms and towns, their loves. He understood their homesickness.

They did not understand his. To them, Estonians were sly, thankless and rebellious children.

But here at the Narva, for some reason the men in the tanks held fire. Were they confused by all that happened back in Moscow this month? Were they more confused by having to face people whose only weapon was song? Were they waiting for a clear order, from a clear leadership?

After *Mu Isamaa,* the Eesti sang a song they had been forced to learn in Russian classes at school. All knew it. And in fact, all loved it, too. A good song with strong harmonic parts and open vowels. A song to pull the heart. *O, The Steppes* by Nikolay Sokolov.

On the other side, shadow men stood behind the tanks, as if listening.

*   *

Hours later, having served his country by leading song, Mikhel hummed another Russian song as he strolled by himself down the main road through the town of Vasknarva, Estonia. His song, *Dark Eyes,* was one he sang only when alone. And today he felt completely alone, alone with his hopes, his fears and his unanswered questions.

Where was justice? Where in all this effort was friendship? In the work to be free, was there even a time and place for love?

This little farming village sat at the north end of the enormous inland lake that his people called the Peipsi Järv. Vasknarva also overlooked the source of the river, the Narva Jõgi, which ran from Peipsi Järv north to the Gulf of Finland.

As Mikhel strolled the road and hummed his love song, he studied the farms, and a lone horse who snorted at him over a fence. He enjoyed the sight of two cows under a cottonwood in a field, and farther down the road near his destination, he saw ancient Mrs. Mannik, weeding her garden while shooing her pampered geese from underfoot.

Beyond the farms, he saw the northern end of the lake waters and the pushing up of bog plants of this teeming countryside.

Over hundreds of years, this bog land had been the scene of struggles by the Baltic peoples to be free of the control of others, especially of the Russians. It had been Mikhel's idea to bring their singing here, to the edge of Estonia, to the town where his mother grew up and where he used to spend summers with his grandparents.

Coming here was an idea that Anja had fallen into as soon as he mentioned it. Once Anja grasped an idea, it became a reality. So, here they were.

The edge of Estonia and the edge of the singing revolution.

Theirs was not the center of the revolution against Soviet rule. The land around the Narva consisted of mires and fens that Russian tanks would not negotiate. If the tanks came through here, they had few roads and one bridge.

Much easier to block one road, when the Soviets ordered troops to remove the singers and take back control of the Baltic lands. Geography worked in favor of the defenders in this time and place.

However, the center of their revolution had always been the Lauluvàljak – the song festival grounds near the capital of Tallinn.

Back in 1987, Mikhel had been as scared and as courageous as he ever wanted to be on that first night. Five years ago. That night, the choir he directed, and all the other choirs in the region went to the festival grounds for the usual Soviet version of their traditional song fest. As in the fifty-two previous years of Soviet rule, they dutifully sang the Soviet approved songs – the songs that extolled the great human experiment that was Soviet life, the songs that pretended the experiment was not a failure, songs that tried to convince the people that truth was not truth, that greed had not entered into the great communal ideal.

On that night, after the official festival ended, the Soviet organizers began to pack up their batons and their music books. But the last song traditionally sung was in Estonian. *Mu Isamaa on Minu Arm* rang out over the festival grounds. But its ending was only the beginning.

By silent agreement, the choirs and the people on the grounds continued to sing. Suddenly the Lauluvàljak, the outdoor festival grounds, swelled with the songs of their grandfathers – the songs they had learned at home and were never allowed to sing in school. That night, they stayed. Stayed all night, singing the forbidden songs in Eesti.

Amazed that no one shot them, or tried to stop them, they just kept singing. Ten thousand packed the festival grounds for nights on end, singing and waiting for someone to bring on the guns.

The guns did not arrive. Night after night, they sang. And the power grew, giving voice to longings, which until those nights, they had only whispered.

Again, they sang forbidden songs in every festival and occasion during that year. And in the following year, 1988, in September, at the Lauluväljak, with 300,000 present, Trevimi Velisti, the Director of Estonian Heritage, had voiced their demand for freedom.

What courage, Mikhel thought. Velisti speaking out the truth. All of us together, singing. What power song and poetry has to bring us out of our bland apartments and into the light of waning summer.

This demand for freedom, non-violent and in music, happened also in Latvia and Lithuania during those years. All the people, angry at the years of Russ infiltration, Russ control, Russ privilege and most of all Russ language instead of the beautiful and honored stories, poems and songs of their own.

And during those years, his Anja, his life friend, had read her poetry on Eesti Raadio and on Raadio2. Her stories and poems about land, family, freedom, were published in underground Eesti newspapers, and she was fired from her job on the Palmse Manor estate where they had grown up as children of servants.

She had become a waitress in town, and continued to write at night, so they didn't see each other often, but whenever his choir sang, she was there with her lyrical voice and beautiful smile. She was the reason he continued to conduct, despite the censors and the sour-faced autocrats who tried to dictate what his choir could do.

Then, the most amazing thing began happening in 1989. At a call from friends, his choir, all the choirs of Tallinn and of the countryside, began to line up and sing along the main road out of Tallinn toward Riga the capital of Latvia. Every Estonian adult and child sang. All belonged to some kind of choir.

The road they targeted was the center of all traffic among the Soviet-run countries of the Baltic. Clogging up this road was a huge and frightening decision.

Mikhel's ema, his mother, had called him from the Palmse Manor, just before he left for the road. "This is dangerous, my son. You can be killed."

"Ema, I have to do this. I would rather die singing than accept Soviets any longer."

She had sighed. Then she whispered, "Your father says you must sing. He wishes you well."

Mikhel swallowed. His father, Ivar Krichevsky, a Russian guard at Palmse Manor, wished him well. "Tell Father I sing for him."

"We sing, too, in the kitchen at Palmse." She whispered. "Now we will sing loud. We will sing with you."

Frightened, and also proud of her, Mikhel had laughed. And then he had said, "Jah, Ema. You sing. I will tell the choir that you do."

"Tell Anja, also," she had said.

That was how he knew even his ema knew how much he cared for Anja. Too bad, Anja never seemed to know it. Still, Anja had come with them to block the road and sing in that year.

Overnight, it had seemed, there were millions along the road, until the millions stretched six hundred kilometers to Riga in Latvia, and from Riga south to Vilnius in Lithuania. Hand in hand, the Baltic people would sing and die, or sing to freedom.

And they had continued to gather and sing to mark every important occasion in the next two years. Now, in 1991, along the fields near the road to Riga and Vilnius, the Russian battalions who were deployed within the Baltic countries brought out their tanks. They faced the two million singers. And for some reason, no one shot or moved on them.

Yet.

Mikhel knew he had to be with the singers. Never would they have another chance to earn freedom. And he knew this land near Vasknarva, so he had encouraged his choir and several hundreds of others to come to this border town to protect the road that led from Lake Peipsi into northeastern Estonia.

Mikhel never fooled himself into believing their revolution had much hope. The singing had gone on for five years. Five years had earned them a stalemate and a face-off, on the road to Riga and also here at the Narva.

Autumn, and little optimism colored the year's move toward another long, dark northern winter. And yet, here they were, the edge of the revolution, and not backing down.

"Jah, boy," old Mrs. Mannik called to him from her front yard. "I see you around here."

He approached her so they could talk across her fence. Her geese gathered at her feet for their conference.

"What is your name?" she asked, twitching her skirt to keep the biggest goose from pecking at her.

"I am Mikhel Aivar." He knew not to trot out his last name. The Russ name, Krichevsky, earned him no points in this border town.

"You tell that girl to stop this singing. She prints these songs. Everybody sings, the tanks gather, and we have no safety and no customers."

He addressed her with great respect for his elders. "I'm sorry, honored Mother. But do you want hardship today, or Soviet rule forever?"

"You dream. We're not getting rid of these Soviets. Tanks won in Czechoslovakia, in Hungary, in Ukraine. Why do you think we can be different?"

Mikhel knew this history. Soviet muscle rolled again and again over the hopes of people. He knew their singing would probably end in death, yet he had to sing for freedom from the everlasting grayness of the Soviet way.

"Ah, but Mrs. Mannik," he said, "Those nations didn't try song. And you know our Eesti. We sing beautiful."

"Boy. You blow smoke, not freedom. I choke on it."

"Hold on, honored Mother. The Russians will come to see that the world watches. In the New York Times, they report every day on our Singing Revolution."

"New York doesn't grow tomatoes and cucumbers on the Narva."

"No. But Moscow wants New York to think it is a gentleman."

"Since when? Get along with you."

"Yes, Mother. May this be over soon for you and for me."

"You might as well invite the Soviets to run over my green house. That's what you are doing here."

"I pray that you live to be free."

"And you as well, Boy. Tell that girl."

"We will talk."

As he walked on down the road, Mikhel Krichevsky thought about that girl who was now a woman. He warmed at the thought, and at the sight of ripe farmland, the green turning to late summer tan in grain fields.

Anja Saarela.

He believed he could not have convinced all these people to come if it hadn't been for Anja's speech at the annual song fest, and Anja's insistent telephoning of her friends and his. She was the draw, the magnet for all.

Anja's poetry was the voice of the Narva campaign. Last spring, she had written a poem she said was especially for him, for the choirs to sing here at the river and the lake. Its one verse became two, because she had written it for him in both Eesti and in Russian.

Cottonwoods Whisper.

At Narva River, cottonwoods whisper

'freedom'

In the mires, a pheasant rushes up

Under the bog, worms remember

Death

Within Lake Peipsi, ice covers valiant knights

Memory lies upon the land, struggling to fly

Both sides of the Narva long for

Peace

Last spring, when she read the poem to Mikhel, he realized that she truly had heard his stories of Grandmother's village, its history of battles and struggle. He had asked her to set it to music and sing her poem for others.

It became her solo at the Laulupidu – the annual song festival, the gathering of the people. By the end of her song, all of Eesti knew the Narva was the next place to take a stand.

Was it any wonder that he loved her more each year?

He looked out over their land. The river, bristled on the near side with camping tents and sleeping pallets hanging to dry. On the far side, there bristled Soviet tanks. On the shore lay sloping sand edged by river willow and struggling rush grasses with geese nests. The geese knew nothing of danger and tanks.

Mikhel had never before so solemnly felt the diabolical predicament that his Estonian mother and Russian father had put upon him. He felt the tension in his shoulders, expecting a Russian sniper to shoot him at any time, on one side. On the other shoulder, his tension was from expecting an Estonian patriot to misunderstand, think him Russian, and knife him.

He had arrived here with thousands of his fellow Estonians. They had spread out, hand in hand, alternately sleeping and then singing in the face of the Russian tanks. The young, the brave, the naïve, hoped that even tank commanders could not bring themselves to shoot a people who sang.

These Estonian dreamers ignored how many died when Gandhiji and Martin King tried the same tactic. All that these young remember is that for Gandhi and Martin it had worked in the long run.

Estonia had declared independence four years ago, in 1988. But it was this moment of military and non-violent truth in 1991 that would create either an independent state, or a massacre of the innocents.

They had come to the time that Gandhi had predicted. "First, they ignore you. Then they laugh at you. Then they fight you. Then …"

The great soul, the Mahatma had predicted, "Then you win."

But they were at the time when next came the fighting.

* *

Recently, in Moscow, an attempted military coup had risen to close off Mikhail Gorbachev from power. The military leaders feared Gorbachev's efforts to release the iron fist from the backs of people, to allow open talk and creative thinking outside the Soviet control. The military wanted to close down what was seen as weakness in dealing with the singers in the Baltic, in the Polish resistance, and in all other bids for democracy and freedom.

Then, crowds of Russian protesters had entered Moscow square, refusing to allow that the military had any right to clamp down even on Russian hopes. The crowd had brought about the return of Gorbachev from house arrest in the south.

But Mikhel did not believe either the military leaders, the party leaders, or that two-faced Boris Yeltsin had given up on stopping the peace that Gorbachev had struggled to bring about.

Could Gorbachev, who controlled the military at this moment in Moscow, also control them as far west as the Narva River? Could the world pay attention long enough to keep these tank commanders in the eye of public judgement?

All lay in the balance.

And Mikhel knew that singing was power, but it was only the beginning. Friendship and love – those were even more powerful.

Included among his compatriots who came with hope, who sang for peace and freedom were many full-blooded Russians who had long ago tired of the pretense that the Soviet system wasn't rigged for the few.

These Eesti-Russians knew that with any return to the Soviet system, the masses, the ones now hand in hand at the border, and also those standing in the square in Moscow, would have to make do with very little. If they didn't stand and sing for freedom, they always would have to salute as they paraded past the grandstands set up for the few.

The few, who always pretended to represent the many.

So, in the many who had come to the Narva, besides singing Estonians, the singing revolution included tired, demoralized Estonian Russians.

Moreover, there was Anja Saarela of the dark eyes and the lovely voice. She, beyond all reason, had encouraged this venture, had traveled here in an ancient Skoda automobile to help lead the songs and pass out the song books. She had brought a printing press in the trailer behind her auto, and had picked up Mikhel on the way, because he could wave his arms in front of a choir, and also, he could run and maintain the press.

They had driven out of Tallinn on the Tallinn-Narva Maantee. They had passed Estonia's huge radio and television transmission tower and the always Soviet-guarded coast of the Baltic Sea.

They had passed through the Lahemaa open and parklike area and the Palmse manor house where his parents still worked for Soviet overseers. They had passed Illumägi Chapel and Cemetery, where Anja's favorite Uncle Jarve, mentor to all the children of the estate, recently had been buried. They left the Baltic and had driven their printing press southeast to his grandmother's old town on the Narva.

And here, at Grandma's native house, he printed for Anja, conducted his ragged, cold, but hopeful choir of freedom fighters. Here, when he was not working, he prayed not to be shot.

Paper, they scrounged. Those who had it, freely brought it. But paper, as with everything in Estonia, was always in short supply. Anja used paper for encouragement – broadsides that helped the farmers bring food to the camping singers, broadsides that brought blankets and sweaters. Broadsides that reminded singers of moving songs in both Russian and Estonian (though some refused to sing the Russian songs).

To those who refused Russian, Anja announced, "My friends, we are singing to convince the tanks to miss their home. We are singing to remind the tanks that mother awaits them, prays for them, makes borscht for them. We must sing to them in Russian. They won't remember mama in Estonian."

Mikhel strolled past one more greenhouse filled with tomato and cucumber plants.

He turned left off the Johvi-Vasknarva road into what seemed to be a work shed, all that was left of his grandmother's neglected home. Inside the work shed, his bed lay at the back wall, neatly made of layers of cotton and wool that his mother had hastily sewn into a pallet for him. The bed was on a deep shelf that once held machinery parts. The shelf kept him from sleeping on the cold concrete floor.

The machine parts now sat on the ground waiting for machinery to need them. Harvest machinery did not move much around Vasknarva this year.

Near the bed, stood a small pot-bellied, wood-burning stove with today's meager soup simmering on top. The stove burned bog peat – wood being in short supply in bog country. The chimney rose up the back of the garage. A supply of peat lay in a stack, drying, he hoped, in the chilly heat of the room.

The stove also had to heat the room in the lean-to attached to the back of the garage, the room where they stored clothing for those who had not come prepared to stay.

Mikhel knew the pot-bellied stove also heated much of the outdoors. He had seen the changing color of the air around his temporary garage home – the color of escaping heat on the rise.

The printing press of the revolution stood on a make-shift table of sawhorses and plywood. A list of "things to print" lay beside the press. Anja's handwriting. Mikhel caressed the note, and then sat down at the typewriter to create the template for yet another broadside. This one plead with the Estonian patriots to respect each other, Russian and Eesti alike.

Anja had written, 'We, together, are fed up with Soviet rule. Soviet rule is not Russian rule. It is the rule of the Party leaders who love power."

Anja would have a hard time convincing Estonians that most Russians who lived in Estonia were not part of that party leadership group. Russian citizens always seemed to be first in line for apartments and first in line for bread.

It was not apparent to many Estonians that only a few Russians were always first in line. Simple guards like his father never had privileges given to the party families.

As Mikhel typed, the garage door opened again. Mikhel turned, hoping to see Anja. But the hulk who stumbled into the garage was a new fellow with wild red hair and frightened eyes.

Yet, he wore the uniform of a Russian tank commander.

Mikhel stood, searching the room for any weapon. The printing press sat stolidly at his left hand.

"I've defected," the man said in Russian, and slumped to the floor. "Please."

Stunned, Mikhel couldn't gather the concept.

The man tried again, in very stilted English, "Please help me. I cannot go back."

Understanding at last, an idea came. "New clothes," Mikhel said in Russian.

The man raised his head to stare. Finally, he said, "Yes."

At last, Mikhel began to think again, and asked in Russian, "How did you know to come here?"

"I saw you. You hand out papers. I followed. I thought, he leads here. He will know what to do."

"Defect? Why?"

"All is chaos in Moscow. Gorbachev is in power for the moment, but the army will soon oust him – as soon as the mob in the square goes home. And then, the generals will return to the border."

"And if they return, you will be hunted."

"I mean to be in the west by then."

"Better improve your English, if that's what you want."

"I was only allowed school until age fourteen, then army."

"I have clothing in the back room. Not much fits you."

The man tried to stand, but slumped again.

"What is your name?" Mikhel asked.

"Ilya Krushchev."

"You're kidding."

"Unfortunately, I am not."

"Might as well be Josef Stalin."

"Not that bad, surely."

Mikhel shrugged, "Maybe not. But you need a new name."

The man smiled at last. "I could be Imre Nagy."

Mikhel remembered the name. Nagy had been the Hungarian prime minister and freedom fighter. Imre Nagy was promised amnesty and then murdered by the Hungarian Soviets.

"Imre, maybe," Mikhel said. "How about Imre, but a common Russian family name?"

Ilya/Imre nodded. "Asimov?"

Mikhel cocked his head. "You read Science Fiction?"

"In Russia, we live in science fiction. To understand our own lives, Asimov is famous in underground print."

"Anisimov?" Mikhel suggested. "Not so obvious."

"Imre Anisimov, then." The man seemed to be rolling those syllables around in his head.

"Imre, why are you weak?" Mikhel asked in Russian.

"I crossed the border six days ago. I hid in the woods south of here."

"You had water?"

"Yes. From the lake. And one slow fish, maybe already dying."

Mikhel went to the pot-bellied stove and ladled soup into a bowl. "This will start you. Then crackers."

The man took the bowl from him, bowed his head and said, "Blessed is He who creates the fruit of the ground."

That phrase startled. "Religion?"

Imre seemed shaken, then shrugged. "Habit. Mother was a secret believer."

Now, much began to make sense. Orthodox? Catholic? Any belief, and you'd want out of the system.

Mikhel watched as the man inhaled the soup. When Imre had finished, Mikhel took the bowl and handed him five crackers. "More later. Let that settle in your empty bowels. I don't understand one thing. How did you become a commander?"

Imre gazed at his uniform. "Oh. The commander died. I fit his clothes."

"You command no one?"

The man grimaced and scratched his neck. "Not even the ants in the grass."

"Can you stand now? I want to get you in the back room in case anyone comes while I'm looking for clothes." Mikhel took the man's arm and helped him stand. They stumbled toward the back room.

In the clothing storage, they found a shirt that fit and was even too big. Pants were harder. Few gave up pants that might last another year. The pants they found were four inches short, but socks filled the difference.

"Here is a jacket. Probably as large as we'll get."

"Where did I come from?" Imre asked, shrugging into the short sleeves. "Some Russian-speaking town in Eesti, maybe?"

Mikhel hauled down a map of Estonia. He turned to the side with the port city of Tallinn. "Memorize the streets of this city. You don't get out much. You wished to go to university in Tartu, down south, but couldn't afford it."

"I know Tartu a little. Where is Tallinn's market?" Imre asked.

"Here. Near the city center," Mikhel pointed, "Between Pikk and Vene, where the tourists gather."

"Music?" Imre asked.

"A lot of music."

"Good. That's good. Where do I live?"

"Out beyond," Mikhel pointed. "Find Mere Avenue. You are in an apartment beyond that, on Ahtri, building two hundred."

"Do I have an apartment number?"

"Number fifty-five. That puts you in a hallway near my apartment."

"There is no fifty-five? I will not implicate a stranger?"

"No fifty-five. Why music?" Mikhel asked.

"I sing in the Army chorus. The only English I learned after school is from the Beatles and Bob Dylan."

"No wonder your cadences."

Imre hung his head. "That bad?"

"Charming, and mercifully not Russian tinted. Want to learn a new song?"

On the spot, Imre burst into

> "Veel kaitse kange Kalev,
> "Oma lapsi ja öpeta,
> vaid vahvalt võitlema,
> Ning Linda, ema ..."

Imre continued singing until eagles' wings took the shackles from the Eesti people.

Mikhel had stopped folding clothes. "Where did you learn that?"

"I listened to your naïve ones singing at the border. I know it talks of your hero Kalev and his wife, Linda, and freedom for Eesti, but I don't understand the rest."

"Kalev and his mother, Linda, founders of the Eesti peoples." Mikhel said.

"Mother, then. I read about them in Moscow library."

"You were allowed to check out books about Eesti history?"

"I was allowed to re-shelve books others checked out."

"Ah. Imre you are resourceful."

"Can you teach me another song?"

"Come out by my printing press and we'll learn Eesti Lipp – about our flag of freedom. When you know that, you can join the singers on the border."

Imre hesitated. "They will know I am Russ," he said. "And on the other side, they will know me by my size."

"We have Estonian Russ among us. But we're cutting off that wild hair and finding you a hat."

*   *

An hour later, much of Imre's red hair lay in the garbage. Hair and his uniform had been incinerated. He and Mikhel sang *Mu Isamaa on Minu Arm* over and over again as Imre ran the press and Mikhel typed. Imre had a deep bass voice, which contrasted nicely with Mikhel's baritone.

Anja Saarela entered the garage and stopped. Her dark hair shone in the momentary light of the open door. The door swung shut behind her.

Mikhel stood. "Anja, meet my neighbor, Imre Anisimov."

She stood still and said, in Russian, which all Estonians had been forced to learn in school. "You smell of the forest and the bog. You've been hiding?"

Imre glanced at Mikhel. And then he, too, spoke Russian. "Miss Leader of songs, I have hidden in the forest. Mikhel has been kind to me. He meant no harm."

"You are Russian. From the army?"

"I . . ."

Anja waved her arm to shush him. "I don't want to know more. Where is your uniform?"

Mikhel said, "In the incinerator out back. It is completely gone."

"Good. You are Imre."

"Imre Anisimov."

"And you speak Eesti?"

"I only sing in Eesti, not speak."

"And in English," Mikhel added, "the Beatles and Bob Dylan. A multi-linguist in song."

Anja stared at Mikhel. She spoke to him in Estonian. "You know that some Eesti already question the dedication of the Russian members among us."

"Including wondering about me," Mikhel said.

"You put yourself in even greater danger with this Imre."

Mikhel gazed at her as at a new person. She had never before worried about his safety. She had counted on his help: type, run the machine, repair the machine, hand out the leaflets with her, wave his arms for the choirs. "Anja, I am as Eesti and as Russian as ever. Why worry about me now?"

"I could speak for you when things became tense at the meetings, but you add this fellow, and all will question. Is he a spy?"

Mikhel froze. "You have had to defend me?"

Anja came closer. "They are nervous. Everyone is nervous. They want to be brave, but the first thing out of their mouths is 'This or that one is not fully committed.'"

His anger flushed his face. "If I had stayed in Tallinn, or in Palmse, they could question my commitment. But I am here. All the Eesti Russians who are here are committed. How can they dare to question?"

Imre spoke in perfect English.

"All the lonely people
Where do they all belong?"

Mikhel and Anja both glanced at him.

"Eleanor Rigby," Imre explained, then said in Russian. "Do you know why she keeps her face in a jar?"

Mikhel wondered if this were a real question, but Anja said. "In case someone comes who might listen to her."

"Yes, she waits for someone," Imre answered. "In the tanks command, no one comes near. No one will hear."

Mikhel stared at his new friend. He made a wonder of the little English he had learned from the Beatles.

Anja asked, "But will they hear us if we sing in Russian?"

"Some will hear. Some will care, but they will always do what the generals tell them to do."

"So," Anja said, "We have to sing for the English newspapers, too."

Imre shrugged. "I don't know who pays attention to the English newspapers, but our men in the tanks do join the Russian songs. Have you heard them?"

Anja nodded toward Mikhel, as if to say, 'I told you so'. "We have not heard. Maybe they need to come out from behind the tanks."

"They fear snipers."

Mikhel said, "So do we."

Imre lifted his pale eyebrows. "But you stand right out there on the banks of the Narva."

Mikhel said, "How else to face down the other?"

Imre sat down hard. "Maybe not so very other."

Anja said. "Pretty much 'other', when you bristle with armor and long guns."

Imre nodded. "Yes. Soon as I swam across, I saw what we look like."

Anja sat next to him. "And what did you think then?"

"I marveled that so many could be so brave. We could run those guns down in one minute, shoot up and down the line and then barrel across the river."

Mikhel said, "You have pontoon bridges waiting?"

Imre nodded. "And snipers. It will take only a word from Moscow."

Anja stood. "I need to check that incinerator. Mikhel, would you come with me?"

Imre sat, watching as if he understood that Anja wanted a private conference. Mikhel raised his eyebrows at the man, and followed Anja out back.

Once there, she opened the incinerator barrel and poked around in the fire, as if that were really her purpose. But she said, "You remember the Russians autocrats who ran Palmse?"

"Of course. I lived there, too."

She continued poking about. "When I was three or four, I touched one of their paintings," she said. "A beautiful lady in a gown of silk. I wanted to know what silk felt like and was too small to know paint was not what it portrayed."

"I remember the portrait, in the library."

She nodded. "The paint was thick and dry – nothing like silk."

Mikhel smiled, remembering Anja as a willful and curious little girl. He had always been afraid for her because curiosity got servant children in deep trouble.

She stood, turned toward him and said, "A woman came into the library and found me standing on the chair. She was dressed in silk – for the evening guests. She had me whipped for daring to touch."

Mikhel felt his heart turn in his chest. How could a woman, even a pampered and selfish woman do that to a little one?

Anja had been such a slight child, the one among his playmates he always wanted to protect. But she never accepted protection.

"Her dress was as thick and dry as the paint." Anja said. "And so was the makeup on her face."

She closed the incinerator and held out her ashy hands. "I marked her dress and her face with fireplace dirt. She went to dinner not knowing."

Mikhel smiled, but then he grew puzzled. "Why are you telling me this now?"

"Imre is a danger, but he is not dry paint. He is what he seems. When we sing, keep him in the second row, behind someone tall."

"I will."

"And Mikhel . . ."

"Yes?"

"Did you ever again get to touch the music box?"

He remembered that curiosity at Palmse, hidden away in a back hall, a thing of noisy promise that no one ever heard. Except that he had touched it, and been beaten with a belt buckle.

He said, "I once touched the little drum, and the cymbals. But I never tried to make it play."

"It doesn't work," she said. "It looks so tempting, but crank as you might, it will no longer play."

"How do you know that?" As soon as he asked, he knew that at some point, she had cranked on it and suffered for the effort. He felt the stripes on his back flare into remembered pain.

"Uncle Jarve tried to get permission to fix it, but the Nazis did not want it to play. And after the Nazis, the Russians wanted it silenced, too."

"Why would they not want it?"

"They wouldn't tell him why. And then they told him to keep me away from it."

Mikhel laughed. "No wonder you drove all this way with all that music and the printing press."

She ducked her head and whispered, "And with my prince."

He stared at her. Had she truly said that? "Anoushka …"

But she had already stepped away. "We must get to the shore, it is our time to sing."

In his confusion, he wondered if he had heard her correctly. As ever, when she came close to him, his mind disordered itself.

*   *

As she opened the door, Mikhel could hear Imre singing a bass part to Eesti Lipp. The man practiced his Estonian and the song about a homeland, not his home, but his wish. In Imre's efforts, Mikhel could hear how much the man longed to belong to something hopeful, something greater than the everyday effort to earn a roof and food.

He knew that same longing himself, but it had more to do with Anja than Eesti. Anja, brave, foolish, lovely and untouchable – his homeland.

Anja strode inside the garage, humming her part in the song. Imre glanced up, kept singing and smiled at her. Toward Mikhel, he raised his shoulders with a question on his face.

Mikhel decided to answer the simplest of the possible questions. "The uniform is gone."

"And me? Should I be gone?"

Anja answered. "Get ready to join us singing. You sing like that and others will accept you."

"But," Mikhel added. "We think you should stand behind someone tall, in the back row. The tank men may still recognize you. Your eyes ..."

Imre nodded. "I know. My eyes show so much white. If you have a sniper rifle, with a sight, you will not miss them."

"So, pull down that hat," Anja said. "Let the bill shade your eyes."

* *

At the river's edge, the tanks began moving back and forth, as if determining which among them deserved first place in line. At the first sign of motion, the singers fell back.

Some tanks pulled back, others thrust into their place, but none seemed to change the high angle of their gun, so Mikhel thrust Imre into the back row of singers and then he strode toward the front, turned and raised his hands as if to conduct this enormous choir. He began singing *Mu Isamaa*, the song even the Soviets must know by now.

He heard Anja's voice from his left and in the back, Imre's bass, then other singers regained confidence.

On the other side of the river, the guns still pointed at the treetops. If all remained calm, only the sky and the cottonwood trees at the edge of the wetlands might suffer shot.

On the tanks that had pulled back, men climbed out. Each sat on top of his tank. Rifles across their laps, they watched the singers.

Mikhel's conducting was no longer needed, so he stepped into the front line near Anja.

All up and down the river, they sang every verse of Eesti Lipp, and then Anja began the words to the Russian folk song, *There's a Little Birch in the Meadow*. Imre took up the opening and though he stood in the back row, the singers around him, backed up out of respect for his strong and beautiful voice. In an effort to keep him hidden from those across the stream, Mikhel and Anja stepped in front of him to sing the solo of the second verse.

Across the Narva, they could hear the voices of those who sang with them. When the song had finished, no tank moved. Several of the men who sat on top wiped their eyes.

So Mikhel began singing Kalinka-Malinka. After his baritone introduced the pleading solo, men on both sides joined in. The song always leads into a fast dance. Somewhere on the other side, a balalaika strummed the joyful rhythm.

As the fun came to an end, Imre began singing Kalev ja Linda. His voice, so deep and strong, again drew attention from the Eesti and the Russ sides. Anja turned to Mikhel and whispered, "Get him further back. They will know him by his voice."

"You come in on the refrain," Mikhel whispered to her as he moved to give Imre cover.

Even as Anja began singing, one of the tanks began to change the angle of its gun. The turret moved toward the three of them, and then down, slowly down.

"Move way back, Imre," Mikhel said.

"Eesti will call me coward."

"If you stay here, that tank will be assured it is you," whispered Mikhel. "They only wonder now. In a moment, they will be certain."

Imre allowed Mikhel to move him back. The gun angle on the tank lifted, but in that moment a big Eesti acquainted with Anja confronted them. "Who is your Russki friend?"

The man had been drinking, so became belligerent and hate-filled toward foreigners.

Mikhel spoke in Russian, so Imre could understand. He knew Peder also understood, however dimly in his drunken state. "My neighbor, Imre Anisimov. Imre meet Peder. Peder's family got stranded here when Poland left." A barb. Almost no one in Estonia could claim pure blood.

"Your neighbor?" Peder asked. He turned on Imre. "Where are you from?"

"Tallinn, out beyond Meer." Imre said, easily. He was a quick study.

"Jah," Mikhel said, "Out in the same Eesti-Russ area where I live. Ahti."

Peder said, "I don't trust you, Krichevsky, and I certainly don't trust this giant." With that, Peder swung at Imre, making him step back into the marsh grass. Mikhel grabbed Peder's arm and twisted. Peder couldn't move. His shouts brought attention, but no action.

Anja brushed Mikhel's grip aside. She stood between him and Peder. Peder rubbed his sore arm. Anja spoke in a low voice.

"Peder!" She waved toward the singers who merely stared at him. "See how you are ignored? You don't trust anybody. Therefore, nobody trusts you."

Peder put his hands out in the time-honored gesture of the innocent soccer player. "But, Sweetheart," he whined, "you've known me since we were nineteen. You can trust me."

"Certainly not. I know it is you who has been hanging around outside my tent and I've told several people that fact."

"I can't help it if my tent is close to yours."

"I moved, and then you moved again. Leave me and my friends alone."

Peder backed off. "Your friends smell of Russki treason."

Two Eesti friends grabbed Peder by the shoulders and hustled him away. One turned back to Anja. "We're moving his tent away from you."

"Thank you," Mikhel mouthed. He watched Anja pull Imre off the wet stubble of the field. Mikhel realized Imre's hat had been knocked off, so he grabbed it up and put it back on Imre's head.

As he turned around, he saw a flash of glass from across the river. Was that binoculars? A gun sight?

He pulled Anja over the incline and below the high levee at the river's edge. Imre was already ahead of them walking down into the field.

Anja pulled back. "Why are you yanking on me, Mikhel?"

"Binoculars. We need to get all three of us down river so whoever suspects or wonders, is not aware we've moved."

"Okay. But if Imre sings, somebody will notice."

"True. We've got to get him on the road to Tallinn," he said. "He wants to get to the west. Might as well start soon."

She nodded. "He's too conspicuous here."

"Tomorrow. We'll need to take him in the car with us and hope there's a freighter he can sign onto. Maybe to Hiumaa or Saremaa. In those islands he could work the fields until . . ."

"Until the Soviets stop wanting to control the whole world?" Anja hissed.

Mikhel had never heard her so angry and defeated. He touched her shoulder. She turned to him, her exhaustion plain in her posture, and her frustration in her defiant gaze.

He pulled her into his arms. She surprised him, and came easily. He said, "I want you to sleep with the press in the garage – away from Peder."

"Will you stay there, too?" she whispered.

"I am always there." He said, and then, for the first time in his life, he had the courage to kiss her.

She had always been so certain, so determined, so dismissive of his offers of protection, but this time, she put her arms around his waist and pulled into him. He knew at last that she must be very tired and discouraged.

Yesterday, this would never have happened.

Then, he began to think about her safety, and Imre's. "Where shall we put Imre?"

"In my tent," she said. "I will sleep with you."

She might as well have sledge-hammered him. For a moment, he couldn't believe. It sounded so simple, but Mikhel knew it would be the complex beginning of a complex life. He also knew he wanted her complications and had always wanted them. Lively, curious, sometimes furious, but always loyal to the ones she loved: Her family, her pets, her damned stingy housekeeper of a mother, her mechanic uncle, her idea of Estonia.

But now, was she pledging loyalty to that half Russki bum, Mikhel Aivar Krichevsky? Or was this a move she would regret tomorrow?

*   *

They moved her tent, cleared her things from it and took her blue and black Eesti flag from its front pole so that the tent would look like all the other Army-resale tents in the fields. All the while they listened to the singing at the river and watched that Imre stayed well below the levee. When they joined the singing again, they also stood below the levee, near their new friend. As the sun fell, Mikhel could not keep his mind off of the coming night and the possibilities in what Anja had said to him. They joined the others for shared tomato soup and bread, the normal fare for so many in a place where there was little game and no market.

As the sun set, Mikhel showed Imre the tent and the blankets they had found for him. Then, he let Anja retire into the garage first, so she could set up her situation as she wanted it. He walked around to his friends at the campfires near the shore.

Because of the motion of the tanks during the afternoon, the friends had decided to have more night guards who could warn the sleepers of motion on the other side of the Narva.

Mikhel felt that his friends were well set up. He saw that Peder's friends had moved his tent, but Peder was sitting at a campfire away from the rest of them, brooding. Mikhel was glad he and Anja had taken all identification from the tent they had given to Imre.

When he returned to the garage, he knocked on the door. Anja opened it and stepped back into the half-light of a low propane lamp. She had set up her sleeping mat next to his in the deep shelf at the back of the garage.

He looked at her as he closed the door. "Are you sure?"

She stared at him. "Would I have done it if I weren't sure?"

His laugh was low and tight. "For sure not."

"I put some more vegetables in the soup."

"Where did you get vegetables?"

"From the goose lady. She says you are supposed to tell me to stop singing."

"Ah," he said, and stepped to the pot to stir it. "You are to stop singing."

"Okay," she said. "For eighteen hours."

He glanced up at her. "And then?"

"We sleep tonight, drive Imre to the ferry to Hiumaa, drive back and sing again."

Mikhel stopped stirring. "I must tell you something."

She smiled and sat next to the typewriter. "Go ahead and talk. It will take at least three hours for the carrots to make peace with the broth."

He stood very still for a moment, asking himself if he had the courage to say what he must say.

"Well?" she asked.

He plunged. "I am not going to take you to bed, and then find someone else next week. That is not how I do."

She nodded. "And you want to know how I do?"

He shook his head. "I know you, Anja. You are loyal, if you love."

She stood and came to him. "My prince. You have spent our lives at Palmse, and then in Tallinn trying to take care of me. I don't need care and protection. I need a partner."

"So, you don't need me?"

"Idiot. I love you, Mikhel, but don't ever believe you have to come between me and danger."

"What do I believe, then?"

"Believe you and I will accomplish much together."

He let out a breath he hadn't even known he was holding. "Much together," He whispered. "Anja."

She smiled and then stood on tiptoes to kiss him, a light promise of a lingering kiss.

As he recovered, she turned off the lamp. Their only light was the peat in the stove. When he reached for her, he realized she had already shed her blouse.

* *

August 21, 1991

The next day, in the morning, as they were about to join the line at the Johvi-Vasknarva Road, Anja reached for the door handle and looked over her shoulder at Mikhel.

"Did you know that the Palmse music box is amazing?" she asked.

"It doesn't work, and it has one useless cylinder in it," He said.

She laughed. "It is useless, isn't it? By the way, I have a surprise for you. Two boxes in the attic at Palmse," she said.

He laughed. "Of course you were in the attic poking through boxes. Did anyone catch you?"

"Only Uncle Jarve."

And without further talk, she led the way to the road and the tents in the fields near the river bank.

Mikhel watched her walk. She could be quick as mercury, but this morning, she swayed slowly down the road. He let himself remember the sweet curve of her hips under his palms. What a beautiful woman. Strong, independent and caring. His, at last.

Off to the right, he heard the revving of tank engines, but saw no movement. Mikhel said, "The tanks are restless again."

"Something is going on in Moscow."

"But what? Out here, we can't get news except from St. Petersburg, and who would believe what they say?"

She shrugged. "We need to find Imre. Take him to Tallinn and then to a port."

"Jah. Get news on the way."

In the line of campers, they found Imre climbing out of the tent. As he cleared the sleeping blankets out to fold them, Peder showed up. He leaned into Imre, his jaw tight and his neck red.

"You pissin' on my tree." He spoke Eesti.

Imre straightened, confused.

Mikhel stepped between them. "You got no tree, Hot Head. Be gone."

Peder whipped out a knife, shining in the sunrise. "He's coming out of her tent."

Mikhel held his arms up, hands empty. "Peder, we got tanks across the river. Bigger things are happening."

He shook his knife at Mikhel. "The tanks will run you down, Russki traitor."

"Let's go face them down, and sing," Mikhel began, but Peder stepped in close and slashed. Mikhel felt the slice in his forearm just as Imre grabbed Peder's knife hand on the back swing. In a move so fast Mikhel didn't see it, Imre had the knife and held Peder's arm behind him, locked.

Over Peder's shoulder Imre glanced at Mikhel, a questioning rise in his near-white eyebrows.

Peder screamed, "Russian spy. Russian spy."

Everybody in the campground looked up. A few started toward them, but Mikhel raised his arms. "Peder is drunk again, folks. Can someone take him to sleep it off?"

A couple of Peder's friends started to come over. Imre handed the knife to Mikhel while Peder kept hollering about spies. His friends grabbed him around the waist and hauled him off toward their campfire.

"Come on, buddy. You need food," they said.

As he passed Anja, Peder spat. "Bitch, whore."

She smacked him in the face.

One of his friends said to him, "We're taking you back to Tallinn. You're just a problem here."

"You're all blind. These Russki-Eesti can't be trusted."

Anja ran to Mikhel and pulled up his bloody arm. "Thought so."

"What?" he smiled down at her in spite of searing pain. "You going to rip your petticoat for me?

Imre handed her a strip off his blanket.

She glanced up at him and laughed. "Perfect," she said. From behind her skirt, she pulled a bottle of Vana Tallinn and poured a half cup on his arm. His arm burned. She said, "Now take a swig of this to cut the pain."

He did. "Where'd you get this?"

"Peder's table."

"Let's get out of here," he said.

Anja looked up at him, all the worry and love of their night in her eyes. "You're the one who always needs protection."

He laughed. "This time, anyway."

Movement among the tanks on the far side brought everyone out of the moment. They could hear a radio on the other side, blaring, but incomprehensible. All Mikhel could make out was staccato voices shouting.

On their side, a woman shouted, "Listen." She turned up Eesti Raadio. Mikhel took Anja's hand as they hurried to the tent with the radio. Imre followed them.

The announcer said something about a human chain. Through the static, the next words Mikhel understood were Raadio, Television and tower.

The crowd around the radio hushed to catch the few words that came through.

Mikhel pictured the huge tower on the Baltic coast. "Twelve hours. Standoff. Tanks and soldiers. Human chain. Protect tower. Fire. Oxygen. Halon. Every. Inside."

Mikhel's scalp tightened. He had friends inside the transmission tower. Velo, music producer and announcer for Raadio2 would be there. He knew his friend Velo would be there.

He glanced at Imre and saw that he also tried to make sense of the Eesti, but this wasn't the place to explain in Russian. All that Mikhel knew from college chemistry was that halon gas stopped fire, and it could kill by taking the oxygen. Had they used the halon to keep the soldiers out? Or was that a threat?

Those who threatened would die, too. And they knew it.

At that moment, Eesti Raadio became one huge yelling crowd. In the background at the station, they could hear tanks revving motors.

Everyone glanced at their own tanks on the opposite bank. The soldiers who had been sitting on the tanks now climbed inside. Near Tallinn, the tanks either revved to leave the tower or to attack the crowd.

And what would the tanks at the Narva do in reaction? Revenge? Back off?

Here they had no halon, or any weapons, only song.

So, Mikhel yelled. "Sing. *There was a Little Birch*."

He marched to the bank and began the Russian song. A moment later, Imre and Anja stood next to him. Other voices joined them at the bank. All Eesti and Eesti-Russ singing, as Anja had said, to remind soldiers that mama waited for them.

On the other side, soldiers not yet in the tanks took up the song. Others popped back out. Officers and foot soldiers sang.

Mikhel didn't know what happened in Tallinn at the tower, but something had changed, and something made this moment a unity.

When the song ended, Imre began singing Kalinka-Malinka. As he got to the dance refrain, both sides of the Narva sang and clapped. The soldiers began stamping their feet in rhythm. On the Eesti side, people danced, ignoring the boggy ground to celebrate something, they knew not what.

As Imre began the verse again, an officer on the other side stood forward, pointed a finger at him. Imre stared at the man and kept singing. Mikhel began to step between them, but Imre put a hand on Mikhel's shoulder and stood forward, still singing in that beautiful voice of his.

On the other side, the officer put up his hand, palm out and then waved at Imre before he turned and ordered his men back into their tanks and their marching lines.

Still singing, soldiers piled into their places. On the Eesti *side*, the refrain came again. All down the line of singers, the dancing had stopped, but the song continued. No one knew what to expect.

The tank guns still pointed at the treetops. The tank engines changed into drive gear. All turned to the right. One by one, they followed each other on the road back to the east. On the Eesti side, no cheering began. Only singing, the continued singing of the dance of Kalinka-Malinka, until the last soldier turned right and marched off down the road.

Afterward, all Mikhel remembered was the exhaustion and the questions. What had happened at the transmission tower? What did the Russian tanks know that took them away?

Someone upriver began a song. Mikhel glanced at Anja. They sang *Cottonwoods Whisper*

Anja smiled up at Mikhel and listened as the others sang her song.

> Memory lies upon the land, struggling to fly
> Both sides of the Narva long for
> Peace

They sang both verses. At the end, Mikhel held her in his arms and whispered, "Lydia Koidula will be proud of you."

She laughed.

*   *

Many decided to stay, just to make sure the tanks didn't come back. There were promises to come back at any sign of Russian muscle. Others needed to go home, to make sure all were safe in Tallinn, Tartu and every small village between.

He, Anja and Imre folded Anja's tent. They didn't see Peder anywhere, and were relieved, thinking he must be sleeping off his drunk of the night before.

They carried the tent to the garage. They packed the press and the paper storage into the trailer behind the poor overworked Skoda.

They were about to pack their clothes and gear when Peder came in the door. He could hardly walk, but he pushed his bulk past Imre and Anja, and saw the two sleeping pallets in the warm shelf.

He turned on Mikhel. "So. It is you."

"Anja and I are to be married when we get to Tallinn," Mikhel said.

"You think so?" Peder raised a gun.

Anja screamed. Peder started to turn toward the sound, but she kicked him in the back of his knees. He toppled to the floor. The shot echoed in the garage and in Mikhel's head even as he pulled Anja away from the man. Imre flattened Peder to the concrete and took the gun.

In his arms, Mikhel felt Anja become limp. He felt the blood from the wound before he found it. Slumped to the floor with her in his arms, he saw. The worst possible. Below her navel, bleeding fast, like the abdominal aorta. He knew minutes of agony would follow. He had seen it when he served in Afghanistan.

She reached for his face. "Look. Me." She whispered. "Palmse."

He looked at her, but he shouted at Imre. "Doctor."

Imre wrenched Peder to his feet. "Oh," Peder moaned when he saw. "Oh, Anja."

"Get him out of here. Tie him to a post. Doctor!"

Imre yanked Peder outside.

"See me here," she said to Mikhel. "I need you."

"I'm here."

"Palmse cemetery. Uncle Jarve."

Tears formed in his eyes, because he understood. "Yes, next to Jarve. Stay, Anja."

"I want to, but ..." she gestured helplessly toward her wound. "Can't feel my legs."

"I know. It is bad," he said.

"I believe. Mikhel, my husband. Love."

"I love you. Always."

She smiled, but said. "Marry again. Live."

"How can I? You are all."

She moaned, and her face tightened with pain. When it passed, she whispered, "I am part. Another can be yours."

"Never."

"Third leg. More balance." She tried to laugh, but the laugh caught on pain.

Mikhel tried to stop her talk by crooning a lullaby his mother used to sing. It came back to him, slowly. She moaned. He stopped singing and realized her moan was also the lullaby. He sang again, with her, holding her still.

"Palmse," she said, when the lullaby ended. "Boxes."

"I know," he said. "The surprises."

She nodded. "And other things."

"We'll look, when we get back," he said, pretending he believed she would be there with him.

The garage door opened. Imre shoved in followed by a Russian doctor and a policeman.

The doctor sank down beside Mikhel. He touched Anja's abdomen. Both of them knew that most of the blood was inside of her. He glanced at Mikhel, who nodded to him.

"Morphine?" the doctor asked.

Mikhel nodded again.

He was barely aware that the policeman went back outside with Imre, but he heard Imre explaining in Russian what happened in the garage. As he watched Anja relax into the morphine, he heard the goose woman come into the yard, complaining about hearing a shot.

The policeman told her all was under control.

Anja took one more breath, and died.

*   *

August 21, 1991

That afternoon, after Imre had put him in the back of the Skoda, Mikhel held Anja's body close to him for the whole trip to Palmse. They had driven, all the time listening to Velo and other announcers on Eesti Raadio, and Raadio2. Of course, Imre had not understood a word, but he had understood that Mikhel needed to know what they might face on the way.

"The tower was saved by the people. The tanks have pulled back everywhere," Mikhel had said.

"Why?" Imre asked. "That is not like the Soviet military at all."

"No, but it may be the coverage from the world press."

"Yes," Imre agreed. "No man wants the world to see his tank run over children."

"Imre learns the way of non-violence," Mikhel said. He spoke to Anja as much as to Imre.

"We are free." Imre said.

Mikhel whispered to Anja. "Imre becomes an Eesti."

Imre said, "We may meet tanks on the road, but we will sit and wait."

After a few miles of open road, Mikhel said, "I want Anja to hear the land."

So, they rolled down the windows and let the August air and the sounds sweep over them. Birds, wind in the trees, and through the villages, the sound of singing, joyful singing.

His mother and father met them. In fact, as soon as they heard his mother crying, all of the servants and many of those who had been overseers came out.

Mikhel introduced Imre and his father quietly took over the job of easing Imre into the staff, while Mikhel carried Anja's body to the dining table.

At someone's urging, a very young man showed up from somewhere near Illumägi church and cemetery, apologizing to Mikhel's mother for his age, and saying he was the closest thing to a priest – a student in religion. Soviet times had not been good to the cries of the human soul.

For Anja's sake, his mother took over the preparations for burial and gently guided the young priest in the old ways.

Mikhel sank to the floor.

* *

August, 1993

Now, two years later, Mikhel had taken over as director of choirs in the village. At Palmse Manor, he had become the head carpenter for the restoration. Soviet times had not been good to beauty either. Palmse had grayed inside and out, and the gardens had become desultory collections of shrubbery and limp vegetables.

One of his first jobs had been to supervise the removal of the barbed wire that the Soviet military had placed along the whole Lahemaa coastline. The Russians had wanted to ensure that villagers had no access to the sea. His father told him he was certain there were land mines near the wire. He had heard talk among the soldiers who laid the wire.

His father was correct.

Mikhel had hired Imre as part of the crew. Imre, it turned out, had a lot of experience hiding land mines, and in Russia, he had given himself an even greater experience by returning to those sites and 'accidently' exploding the same mines from a measured distance. In Lahemaa Park, they heard his timed explosions daily.

Imre, not surprisingly, grew lonely. He told Mikhel that he had followed a sister to Estonia. She had come on a Soviet scholarship to study science. Evidently, she was bright, because, after the revolution, Tartu University kept her on as an adjunct professor and graduate student in botany.

Mikhel was able to get Imre a letter, stating his provisional citizenship in the new country of Estonia. This allowed him to take the old Skoda on a visit to his one family member. He returned from that trip south to Tartu in much better spirits.

Imre learned Eesti quickly and became Mikhel's mediator and right–hand man, making work between Eesti and Eesti-Russ on the crew much smoother.

But Imre wanted a wife. None of the fathers of the Lahemaa Park villages trusted him.

As he said, "They look at the wild red hair and the whites of my eyes, and all they see is a Russian who appears crazy. I can't change how my eyes are built, so no wife."

Mikhel laughed and said, "You are looking in the wrong places, my friend. Look among the red-headed Danes. They tend to have this look of terror, like they shipwrecked here in 1227 and have never gotten over the shock."

"Not funny."

"Yeah, not funny." Mikhel agreed, leaning against the rake he used to find barbed wire in the grasses. "I wish I could be more helpful."

"You don't even feel what I feel," Imre said.

Mikhel looked at him a long time. "You're right, my friend. I'm the wrong person to ask how to look for a wife."

Imre glanced out at the Baltic Sea and sighed. "I'm so sorry. She was wonderful."

*   *

On his off hours, Mikhel had taken the old music box into his Palmse woodshop to fix. Major gears had been taken from it. Mikhel cut new gears based on the pattern of the gears that had been left inside.

Next, he checked the plectra – the sturdy and singing metal strips that were plucked by the cylinder spokes. To his surprise, it seemed someone had cleaned them. They were in remarkable shape.

But someone had stripped many of the musical spokes from the one cylinder that was inside. Still, when he had put the whole thing back together, he could hear in between the missing notes. The song it played was clearly *Die Moorsoldaten*, a song written during slavery of Socialists and Communists in Nazi camps from 1933.

> Far and wide as the eye can wander,
> Heath and bog are everywhere.
> Not a bird sings out to cheer us.
> Oaks are standing gaunt and bare.
>
> We are the peat bog soldiers,
> Marching with our spades
> to the moor.
> We are the peat bog soldiers,
> Marching with our spades
> to the moor.

It did not surprise Mikhel that Nazi invaders stripped the gears and the cylinder for such an anti-slavery, anti-Nazi song. The greater mystery was how such a song ever made its way into the Von Pahlen's manor home.

Who decided to place this cylinder inside the expensive toy that was the Palmse Music Box? An act of defiance, surely.

No wonder, when he was a child, the Soviets beat him for playing with it. Did they beat Anja as well? Or her uncle Jarve?

For weeks, tinkering with the music box became his rest from work and from thought.

After independence, Palmse was the first manor to be restored. His and Imre's crew had worked hard and were proud of the transformation. His father trained the Palmse docents and oversaw national advertising. His mother took over the kitchen of the Palmse restaurant.

Tourists were the income for the whole Lahemaa National Park, and the old Von Pahlen manor house, The Palmse, was now open almost daily. His new bell choirs played, and his choirs sang here on holidays. Imre sang bass in his choir and played the largest deep bells.

But Mikhel's heart would not heal, and Imre knew it. He knew because Mikhel never opened Anja's boxes.

August 21, 1993

This morning, on the second anniversary of Anja's death, Imre had said to him, "It is time."

And at last, Mikhel agreed with him.

Mikhel sat at the upstairs attic window in Palmse Manor. Next to him lay two boxes. In front of him outside the window, lay the manicured lawn, the gazebo, the rebuilt boat house at the shore of the lake. In the distance, the afternoon sun shone on Illumägi Hill, chapel and cemetery.

He imagined the young priest up there, trying earnestly to learn from his neighbors what it meant to be a shepherd.

In the foreground, Mikhel saw a car drive up the hill and turn into the parking lot. He watched Imre stroll out to meet the driver. Out stepped a woman with red-gold hair. She wore the uniform of the park forester. Imre hugged her.

Mikhel smiled, thinking, "Ah, my friend, you have at last been looking at the Danes."

Then he went back to work.

He had come alone to the attic to find the boxes that Anja told him were there. Through all the roof repairs, Imre had kept them safe in the barn so that Mikhel did not have to deal with them.

When the roof had been finished, Imre had brought them back to the attic. And now, Mikhel put his courage into his fingertips and opened the first box.

Inside that box, he found an amazement – cylinders for the Palmse music box. They were numbered. It puzzled him, that numbering system, until he realized that number one was slightly more rusty than number 2 and so forth to the last and shiniest cylinder.

A chronology of cylinders.

In the second box, he found writings from Anja. He stopped, unable to read for the fog in his eyes and in his head. He carried that box to his room, where he placed it on the desk, awaiting further courage.

Then he returned to the attic and took the box of cylinders downstairs and out to his workshop.

On the way out, he saw that Imre was giving his new girlfriend the grand tour of the park around Palmse. Mikhel smiled. Imre's taste in girlfriends had taken an about face. This one was taller and more energetic than his usual.

In his workshop, he opened the box again. All the cylinders seemed unused. They seemed to have sat in the attic un-played. Were they never played?

He settled the first one into its place in the music box, cranked and let it play.

Cylinder number one was a complete recreation of Die Moorsoldaten. After he played it, he inserted cylinder number two. He turned the crank, tightening the spring, and let the music begin again.

Something in the cylinder set off the little drum on the side of the Palmse Music Box. It thrummed only on beat one of each four-beat measure.

The small bells that hung on the front of the box chimed together at the second beat of the second and fifth measures.

When the cylinder's spokes began passing over the plectra, Mikhel recognized music of the Finnish composer, Sibelius, *Finlandia*.

From his mother, he had learned an Estonian version of a hymn written to this tune. Later, he had heard it in English.

My countries skies are bluer than the ocean
And sunlight beams on clover leaf and pine.

When he first learned that poem, he thought it written about his Estonia, but when he was in Afghanistan with the Soviet army, he learned better. Afghanis fought hard.

But other lands have sunlight too, and clover…
And skies are everywhere as blue as mine.

Mikhel had known then that each man loves his homeland. And each wants freedom under his patch of blue.

Die Moorsoldaten? Finlandia? Who planted these cylinders here? And when?

Now, Mikhel wondered what was on these newer cylinders and where they had come from.

He put the next one into the music box, cranked up the spring and listened to *Mu Isamaa on Minu Arm.* He began to smile.

This cylinder had to have been made after 1945 when Ernesaks wrote the tune for the Koidula's poem. When the cylinder wound down, Mikhel sat at his desk, staring at the rest of the unused cylinders.

All new, all without rust and without wear on the spokes.

He stood suddenly and strode to the drawers at the other end of the workshop, the drawers that had always belonged to Uncle Jarve Saarela. Behind the third drawer, he found the old gears and in the very back of the cabinet, in an old box, another set of gears that was new.

Jarve also had fixed the Palmse Music Box. And Jarve had defied the prohibitions and continued the defiance of previous maintenance men, creating cylinders that sang of freedom and of a love so deep that only music could express it.

One by one, Mikhel put the cylinders into the music box. With each one, he listened to the very end – each one a song sung on the road to Riga, in Lauluvaljak, or at the Narva.

After a time, he realized that the maker of the cylinders had become more and more skilled. More four-part harmony and better tone arose from the songs. He stopped and looked inside again.

For the first time, he realized that Jarve had kept the old tinkly plectra, but he had added newer ones as well, more octaves in the little space, longer and shorter for lower and higher tones.

Mikhel plucked the newer ones. Their tone deepened the whole sound. He stared again at the cylinders, put number one back in to play, and watched what happened on the inside. On what appeared to be Jarve's first cylinder, the bog soldiers' reconstruction, only the old plectra were struck by the spokes on the cylinder.

In later songs, more plectra went into action. In those discs, old plectra became the back-ground notes, adding a slightly ancient feel to the newer bell-like sounds.

The thing had become a work of genius.

And every song was a part of the defiance of over-lords begun by *Die Moorsoldaten.*

Jarve had added *Kalev ja Linda,* and even Woody Guthrie's *All You Fascists Bound to Lose.*

The next-to-the-last cylinder began slowly. As soon as the tune started, Mikhel recognized not only Anja's song, but also the tone of Anja's voice.

How could that happen? What had Jarve done to make it so like her?

At Narva River, cottonwoods whisper

'freedom'

In the mires, a pheasant rushes up

Under the bog, worms remember

Death

He bowed his head over the workbench on which sat the music box. His arms were empty. His heart melting. His throat tight with wanting.

> Within Lake Peipsi, ice covers valiant knights
> Memory lies upon the land, struggling to fly
> Both sides of the Narva long for
> Peace

It played twice, just as Anja would have sung it. At the end, Mikhel stood silently for a long time. Then he took the cylinder from the box and, merely out of a need to clear the air, he played the last one.

It started with one melody line for four bars. He didn't recognize it. The next four bars played a full chord with each note, as if something large stomped across the land.

Suddenly, the tune danced for eight measures and danced for those measures again.

Then, the music box played an awful discord. Mikhel glanced up, worried at the cause.

But a last line played smoothly again, the one opening melody line repeated, but this time ending on a second beat, as if unfinished.

He didn't know anything about this song. He took the cylinder out. Saw where the crash chord was built on purpose, and then looked at the last spokes. It did end on a second beat. No spoke had missed its plectra. There was no last note where one would be expected.

Puzzled, Mikhel put the cylinders back in their box. He carried the box up to his room. And then, he went back to the workshop and carried the music box out toward his room. On his last trip, Imre called to him.

He set down the Palmse music box on the driveway, turned, and saw Imre's arm about the shoulders of the girl with the red hair. They walked toward Mikhel.

In Estonian, Imre said, "Mikhel, I want you to meet my sister, Judith. She's working off in those woods." He gestured toward the Lahemaa Park and the Baltic shore. "Forester. Tartu University."

Perplexed, Mikhel stared at her. Then remembered to put out his hand to greet her. "Judith?" He heard the question in his voice. Her grip was firm, and warm from their walks about the grounds.

Imre supplied an answer. "Remember? She escaped two years before me. Scholarship to study science."

"Judith?" Mikhel's voice still couldn't get it together to be normal.

"In Russia, I am Julja. Judith is my real name. Our family is Jewish," She spoke in clear Estonian.

Mikhel glanced at Imre. "And you are Ilya? Right?"

Imre nodded. "Jah. Ilya and Julja. But I prefer Imre. Imre is good."

Judith said, "Ilya means 'worships Yahweh'. Imre, a leader. Fits him." Her low voice seemed as resonant as any he had heard on the radio or in his choirs – a contralto, he guessed.

"Ah," he said. "I'm glad Imre has family here now. And congratulations on your new position."

She smiled, "Thank you. I hear the two of you yanked a lot of barbed wire before I came."

"Yes," Mikhel said, "glad to get rid of the stuff, but be careful. May not have gotten all the pieces."

"We are careful," she said. "Land mines and all the possibilities. One of the things we learned in university."

Mikhel nodded. He remembered Imre teaching him how to detonate the things they found on the shore. She shouldn't be working in those woods. Couldn't Imre tell her that? He stared hard at him, trying to pass a silent message. But Imre just stood there as if there were no danger to her.

"I'll be seeing you around," Mikhel said, shortly. It worried him that he worried about her.

Behind her, Imre smiled at Mikhel. "Good day?"

"Lots of repairs," Mikhel said, gesturing at the music box. He didn't want to talk about what he'd found. Not yet.

*   *

In his room, he set the music box down near his desk and then he strolled across the room to stare out the window at Imre and Judith. They were not twins, though the names Ilya and Julja suggested it. She had dark green eyes, not blue, and her hair was a darker gold than his. Plus, she seemed younger. Had Imre made sure she got to university?

Twins or not, their talk and their walk indicated a love for each other that was deep. He saw her say something to Imre that made him throw back his head and laugh. Mikhel had never seen him do that.

He wondered why Imre had not mentioned she was moving here.

Mikhel walked away from the window to his desk, and opened Anja's box.

At first, he found poems and stories that he had heard her read on Raadio2 and Eesti Raadio. And then essays written for the underground newspapers. He reread each one.

Hours later, in the bottom of the box, he found her poems in a separate file.

Here was the original of *Cottonwoods Whisper*, with strike outs and amendments that showed how Anja thought. He smiled, loving his memories of her quick mind, her urgent curiosity, her fierce independence.

As he read through the poems, he savored the ones she had turned into songs, played on her piano, sung with his choir. And then, he found one he had never seen before.

My Small Country, My Love

None recognize the strength of the small ones
My love, build on small strengths,
Use the tools given you.
Be free, yet understand
The fettered
The fearful.

Teach them truth.
It is the big ones who fall hard.
One kick at the knees
A push,
They shatter.

Teach the fearful truth.
It is the big ones who fall hard.
One kick at the knees
A push,
They shatter.

But the shards of their fall
Are most dangerous.
My Estonia, and my love,
Do not be cut by the shards.
Move beyond . . .

As soon as he read it, he felt the rhythm of that last cylinder. He knew exactly where the crash chord would fit in, and then the unexpected ending.

He realized in that moment that Anja had worked with Jarve on the cylinders, and after Jarve died, she had continued to create them.

He closed his eyes, remembering the moments before her death. Peder and the gun.

One kick at the knees
A push,
They shatter.

In that moment, he finally cried, his head in his hands, remembering their last night and how beautiful her love had been. Minutes passed, tears became sobs and then gasping for air until he became completely worn. He sat there, lost and lonely, finally admitting his grief – a grief that no amount of carpentry and land clearing could ignore.

The shards, he thought. The bullet, her death, my beloved one.

My Estonia, and my love,
Do not be cut by the shards.
Move beyond . . .

Move beyond.

Moments later, he put the last cylinder back into the Palmse Music Box, pulled out his pad of sheet music, and began writing the parts for his choir. He liked what she had done for the bass part. Beautiful for Imre's deep Russian voice. When he finished writing, he played the cylinder again, singing the parts.

In the silence that followed, he heard Judith's full-throated laughter join Imre's outside on the lawn. He stood and glanced out the window. She swung into her car and waved at her brother.

The Other Side
Of The Palmse Music Box

August 19, 1991

I am Madis Ak. I am a colonel in the Estonian army – army, such as we are at this stage in a war to become a country. It is 1991 and my idealist country folk believe they can fend off Russia by singing. A hopeless dream.

At least it gives us time to build a real army.

I stand at the place where the Narva Jogi, or Narva River rushes out of the lake. I stand firmly on the Estonian shore of Lake Peipsi, the Peipsi Jarv as my people call it. Beneath this placid lake surface lie the bones and the armor and the horses of armies who tried to invade our country in times past. The ice – the false and alluring ice.

And today, the ice entices the tanks of Russia. They know the history as well as I. Those in the tanks on the other side of the Narva River do not want to brave this ice. They cannot hope it will hold. They fear an order to move forward.

An officer on the other side of the Narva has come to the shore to study the ice. He wears no helmet, only a warm hat. From beneath the edges of his wool stocking cap, I can see red-blond hair fringing his face. He wields a pike, poking at the edges to gauge the possibilities.

"I would not even try it," I shout to him in Russian. He is not at all surprised that I speak Russian. It is the forced language of fifty years of Russian overlords in our land. They tried but could not kill our Eesti tongue.

He answers me, "Da. Not so solid."

"You are smart to test. Send that information to your commanders."

"I shall. Why do you stand out there? Are you waiting for me to shoot you?"

"No. I'm waiting for you to realize that neither my death nor your death will solve anything. Our people want our land back. Your people want their land back. And both our peoples want the wealthy pretenders to fall into this lake and drown."

"Pretenders, eh?" He glanced back toward his wall of tanks and further toward the fires that heated his comrades.

"You cannot speak it aloud. But we all know. You are here because they are in Moscow plotting how to keep their money and their mansions on the Crimean coast and their yachts."

"Do you like to eat?"

"Indeed," I answer.

"I am Sergey Konstantin Ligachev. I eat at the Hermann Tavern in Narva."

"A good place," I say, wondering, why he is telling me this. Finally, I decide to answer in kind. "I am Madis."

"Madis." He saluted me. "Evidently colonel in a ghost army."

"Da, and you? Lieutenant in an army of marionettes."

"Marionettes?" he glanced back toward the tanks and the campfires. "Marionettes awaiting a change of the pullers of strings."

I thought over the goings on we hear about in Moscow. Has the revolutionary crowd in Red Square been mowed down by those in power? Have the oligarchs killed Mikhail Gorbachev where he is held on the Black Sea coast? Who will yank on the strings of these poor soldiers when this week is up?

I continue shouting. "I am going to turn my back to you and rejoin my people."

"Your people and mine share the same needs," he says, "a roof, food, education."

I turn back and add, "Hope and freedom from lies."

He leaves his pike standing erect in the ice and watches me leave. Minutes later, I find a bog willow where I can relieve myself and also watch that he takes his pike back to his tank.

*   *

I am a colonel in an army that is not supposed to exist at all. According to the Russians, we are radical insurgents and Nazis.

Get that! They describe us as Nazis! What a joke on their people. A country run by the very wealthy who lie to their citizens. They sell them on the idea that they are living the communal dream – and they describe us as Nazis.

Of course, many of their citizens know the truth, but, though they mass in the city squares and yell for the return of leader Gorbachev, they do not have the power to change kidnappings, poisonings, murders, arrests and fake trials.

They cannot change what is happening to the money that should be spent on Russia and Russians. Nor do they have the power to change the state ownership of radio, television and the state newspapers who spread the naked lies, pretending they might convince any thinking person.

There are, of course, Russians within Estonia. The government sends them to run us as serfs. Some Estonian Russians believe the lies. Others, those with less access to stolen money and the perks of being at the top – those who live like the rest of us – they want freedom as much as we do.

I see that Lieutenant Sergey Konstantin has moved beyond the campfires and has jumped into a jeep.

I pull my bicycle from the reeds near the Narva and ride west, stopping every few minutes to listen to the receding voices of singers who block the roads across the bogs and into Estonia.

I know many of these singers, friends with whom I play in a bell choir, or sing the baritone part in a vocal chorus.

Back in Tallin before this singing revolution began, I always believed my friends to be rational and practical people who happened to share my love of music.

Since 1987 – for four years now, they have had this crazy belief that the Russian army will not want to run down people who stand in the middle of a road and sing.

Haven't they seen the film of the massacre in China's Tiananmen Square? Do they think Russia's powerful people have any more morals, or Russian soldiers have any more courage to say 'no' than those leaders and soldiers in China?

I realize after an hour of riding my bicycle that I am headed for the town of Narva and the Hermann Tavern. I have passed many fields of frozen wheat, of dead sunflowers, and multitudes of greenhouses filled with cucumbers and tomatoes, yet with ice on the glass roofs.

Winter is not beautiful anymore. It is as gray as the life we lead, the buildings we live in and the people we meet. Winter is for drinking your sorrows into oblivion and pretending with your friends that you actually wish for tomorrow and its sunrise.

If we had freedom, what would we do with it? We, who have spent almost three generations unable to plan, to think beyond the next meal, to plant what we want and to find even the merest egg without standing in line.

Oh, some of us have just enough land to raise chickens, maybe a pig or two, but raise a life? No. Raise healthy and happy children? No. Raise hell? Raise objections? Raise new ideas? Never.

My friends who sing, raise hope – crazy hope that cannot be realized.

And I have no idea why I am working my way to Narva and the tavern – no idea.

*   *

Ten bicycles rest in the bike rack next to the tavern. Mine is the rattiest, so, unlikely to go missing. I'd take that blue one if it weren't locked up. It looks like it could keep me on the road through nearly any rise in the landscape – that is, if the landscape had any idea how to rise. Our land is so flat that most of it is one long and permanent puddle.

You see a hill? And a mansion on top of the hill? You know that place was probably made by a hundred slaves shoveling dirt sometime around the year seventeen hundred and fifty.

And since that time, hundreds more serfs have kept the mansion – the mõïs – above the bog and maybe kept the roof from leaking, while the ones who live in the mansion have no idea how even to light the stove in the corner of their bedroom.

Our land is flat, below sea level in too many places, and without the beauty it would have had if it were truly our land.

My grandfather's farm once was a lovely place. Now it is useless, and my grandfather is dead and buried in Siberia where these Russian bastards carried him off by train.

When I finally decide to enter the tavern, I don't even lock my bike. I merely let the chain on the next bike hang over my tire as if it were my lock. Who would want such a beat-up vehicle? Not I.

Except that it is my only vehicle. If it were gone, I really would have to steal the next best bad bike standing here.

A colonel without a horse! Ha!

A colonel without an army – with only these arm-waving, throat-clearing dreamers, singing away, and blocking the only road access from Russia for miles about here.

Blocked. So far . . .

My God, it is dark in this tavern. How would I ever know that he is here?

And why do I care?

"Madis," a voice calls out from my left. I turn toward a corner table that is barely visible and see a hulking shadow that must be him.

I approach and by his thick and rather longish red-gold hair, I recognize the man. "Sergey Konstantin."

"Sit. We can order. Cucumbers and tomatoes, of course, and a little chicken – a very little chicken which I suspect is the metamorphosis of a rat."

"Tasty," I say, and I don't doubt that he has read the meat correctly. "Rat, squirrel, dog – could be anything in this time of deprivation and long lines. Chicken – unlikely."

But we determine to order it. And Beer. Always in Estonia there is beer. Sergey Konstantin is sorry that it is not vodka.

"A faster way to blot it all out," he says.

"Blot out what's going on in Moscow, or here at the border?" I ask.

"Blot out my memories of Lahemaa," he says, suddenly switching to a very clear Estonian idiom. "I lived there. I loved it there."

I glance up at him. "You lived in Estonia, in Lahemaa?"

"Nearby. I used to wander into the forest there, until we put so many bombs in the woods to keep the Eesti from wandering down to the shore."

I'm stunned. He knows my home, and I know nothing about him. Yet, the man speaks Estonian as if he were one of us.

"Who are you, really?" I ask him.

"I was the son of the manager of a farm nearby." He reached his hand across the table. I took it.

'Sergey Konstantin Ligachev," he said.

"Madis Ak," I said, "Illumagi."

"So," he said, "Not far from our farm."

The waiter came. He spoke in Russian. "You two friends?"

"Came from the same place," I said.

"Signing a peace treaty," Sergey said in Estonian. "Negotiations underway."

The waiter snorted. "Not likely," he said. "You going to eat or negotiate?"

"We'll eat," I said, "I'll have the chicken-like thing and a beer."

"Same here," Sergey Konstantin said.

"Coming right up," he said.

Sergey returned to our previous conversation. "I imagine you sing in a choir – maybe the community choir out at the ski lodge."

"Why yes, except that they moved that to a renovated barn on an old farm."

"Oh? Why the move?"

I wasn't sure I wanted to tell him. It occurred to me exactly who this guy must be, the son of the Palmse manager, and I knew the Palmse manager wasn't supposed to know about the piano and the barn, or about the choir and the set of tuned bells that were stored there. So, I started to give him a vague answer when the owner brought our order and set it in front of each of us.

Just then, five young men came into the tavern, already drunk from some visit to another location. They saw Sergey Konstantin and his uniform as soon as they came in the door. One member of their crew stumbled on the doorstep and landed next to our table.

Sergey reached down to help him. "Friend, are you hurt?" He asked.

The man rose, looked at our uniforms and spat at Sergey. I stood.

"You again," he said to Sergey "I can't believe you'd come back here."

I said, "Here, I will help you up to move on with your friends."

He glared at me. "What is your place here? Eating with this swine?"

"I am eating dinner in peace and quiet and would like to continue doing that."

"Eat with this Russ pig?"

"Sir," I said, "The only pigs I see here are drunk on somebody else's beer."

The man rose with fists clenched, but our host stepped between us and said to the other man, "I have told you not to return here. I don't want your business."

The other four drunken men in the group surrounded us. But other customers rose from their tables. Instead of leaving the obvious trouble, the other customers surrounded the drinking rowdies.

"Out," ordered the owner.

The other customers took hold of each of the five men and propelled them toward the door.

The man who spat looked back toward me, and said, "The devil take you, traitor. Consort with Russki animals!"

I felt certain he would have said more, but the customers pushed him out and slammed the door.

I returned to our table and sat down. I noticed that the owner had left three beer glasses on our table and wondered why, but the man came back, saying, "I'm sorry. I left my own drink here when they came in."

I handed him the third glass and said, "I'm sorry you have to deal with customers of that sort."

He glanced at Sergey, and said, "There is tension everywhere, and too much drink fuels it."

Sergey nodded, "Friend, I think I am not the type of customer you need at the moment. I won't be back until this is all over and I can come without my uniform."

"Finish your meal, son. I know you haven't a choice about your assignment here. Let us hope this ends without blood being shed."

"Amen to that," I said.

Sergey added, "I hope our friends keep singing until the mob in Moscow convinces that Yeltsin fellow to bring back Gorbachev from his house prison."

I stared at him. "You really believe the singing will do anything?"

He put his elbows on the table and leaned toward me. "I definitely hope so. We've held off so far. Hesitation makes a man think about all he might lose if he leaps across a certain line."

I said, "That mob in Moscow wants exactly what we want – a life free from gray nothing."

"Freedom from Art that is not art," Sergey said. "Music that is not music."

I, thinking of all the words spoken over the nearby Soviet radio tower, added, "Poetry and essays and novels that say nothing, nothing to feed the soul."

Sergey looked at me over his beer stein. "This beer is not as good as his usual."

"A little bitter, to go with the tension of the day."

Sergey glanced toward the door where the five men had been ushered out and said, "Tension of the evening. Thank you for standing up for me."

"You would have done the same," I said.

He shook his head. "There was a time when I listened too much to those who hated Estonians. I would not have stood up for you back then."

"What made you change?"

"I hope I have changed, but the test is yet to come, I fear."

"Yes. At the Narva River we will all be tested. Perhaps we should join the singing and lay down our arms."

"You didn't bring your rifle this evening," he said.

I laughed. "Too heavy and awkward on the bicycle."

Sergey pushed back his reddish forelock and chuckled. "Mine is locked in my tank. Coming across here, I wanted no temptations to use it."

"I don't blame you," I said. "As we saw here minutes ago, a gun would have asked for trouble."

For a few minutes we both ate and enjoyed the warmth of the room and of the other customers who had been such a help. I was pretty certain they were helping the owner and not me or Serge – probably all of them were regulars here. They wanted Alexey, our host, to keep his business going. Their intervention had made a big difference.

Maybe there was hope here at the border after all.

Serge suddenly grabbed at his stomach. "I'm not feeling so great. Must be all the grease I've had to eat in the weeks since we got here. My system isn't used to real meat – rat or whatever."

"Meat or weeks of smokey fires."

"Something. I think I better be on my way," he said.

I stood to shake his hand and wish him well. "I hope to see you once again in Illumagi or at Lahemaa, when we have peace."

He still had a hand protecting his stomach, but he looked me in the eye and said, "May you have a country of your own soon."

"Thank you, my friend."

"Good night, Madis."

He hurried out the door and soon, I heard him starting up his jeep. It bumped its way out of the turnaround and hurried down the road toward the Narva bridge. It occurred to me to wonder if he had found a place to drive across the ice, since the bridge was blocked. I wondered why that thought had not come to me earlier It was possible I would never see Serge again.

*   *

I sat in the warmth of the tavern and finally finished my meal, washing it down with the bitter beer.

At last, I rose and went to the desk to pay the bill for my meal. I hadn't seen the owner for a while but dealt with his helper.

"Where is our host?" I asked, merely out of politeness.

"He had to retire to the back for some business."

"I see," I said. "And do you have a bathroom available?" I had begun to feel full, maybe a little gassy and uncomfortable. With a long bike ride ahead of me, I decided to take the precaution of not having to take a piss in the night at the side of a dark road.

"To the right, at the end of the hall," the helper said.

As I walked down the hall, I felt more and more cramps in my stomach. Just before leaning upon the door to the bathroom, my throat convulsed. I fell into the bathroom, unable to see what I had landed upon, but I felt the legs of another human beneath me, the tile floor and the cold that descended upon me while I could not breathe and could not eject the monstrous bile which filled my whole being. I heard the echo of my own sprawling efforts to throw up.

And then my world became black silence.

* *

Music. Not blessed music – mere cacophony. A cymbal. A drum. A plinking damned indescribable mess of noise that pretended to be a tune.

"He is with us at last," a voice said. The voice seemed pleasant enough, though a bit hollow. Madis thought her voice seemed like the voice of a woman speaking from down the hallway and facing away from him.

"Turn it off," Madis shouted, but then realized he had said nothing, merely thought it. So, he tried again.

"Turn that damned thing off."

"Oh," a second voice laughed. "I think he means the music box. "Stop cranking it, Jergen. If you are trying to annoy Sergey's mother as she leaves us, you may as well know, she cannot hear it."

The third person, Madis thought he must be Jergen, said, "She is not even taking Sergey with her."

"His orders," the voice said. "He has not allowed her that final indignity."

"How about this one? Wasn't he the son of the priest, back when we had a priest?"

"Pastor. It is very different." The woman's voice said from far away."

I thought, "Are they discussing me? My father? The Soviet bastards took him away with grandfather. Grandfather died while my father held him in his arms."

"Just lay all three of them next to each other, they will become one of us in a moment."

Madis was so tired, he didn't even wonder who they were talking about anymore. He merely slept.

What seemed days later, he became able to open his eyes and gaze around him a bit. He did not recognize the place, but then, he thought, "I do not know Narva all that well. I could be in someone's home near the Fort Hermann, or near the Tavern Hermann."

Yet what he saw about him did seem familiar – worn fabric, wall paint so dull it seemed to be apologizing for its own existence, carpet worn so that in some places only the warp was left to hold it together. He lay in a home that Soviet times had entirely neglected – so maybe an Estonian home. But the biggest question then presented itself. What Estonian in Narva would take him in?

Indeed, what Estonian in any town would take him in.

Then he remembered the mention of a pastor, the speculation that his father had been the pastor. Could he be in Illumagi?

Illumagi, where the church had become a storage house for weapons after they took his father away?

No. Not Illumagi.

Moreover, he thought, there was no house this big in all of Lahemaa except the Palmse – maybe a couple of other manor houses, but he remembered nothing this big.

So, how did he get from Narva to Lahemaa and possibly into the Palmse?

Did not some voice say the manager's wife was leaving?

And what had that voice said about Sergey? Was this his friend, Sergey? He tried to move, to see more.

And there, on a carpeted floor, next to him, lay Sergey, asleep. And beyond him, the host of the tavern.

What brought him here?

Madis sat up. He poked Sergey's shoulder. "Sergey. Lieutenant. We seem to be home. Or some place very like home. Wake up."

Sergey rolled over. He opened his eyes and stared at Madis.

"Turn it off, for God´s sake!"

Madis could not hear the awful machine this time, but he felt that must be what Sergey talked about. So, he said, "Jergen, stop cranking it. Where is it?"

No one answered him. Sergey looked up at him. "Thank you. That thing should never have been brought upstairs."

"What thing?" Madis asked.

"Never mind. It is off, at least."

Madis frowned, unsure what to think about the noise they had both heard, but at different times.

Sergey grasped Madis´s hand. "How did you find me?" he asked. "I was in a ditch and water kept coming in until . . . I thought I would drown. I could hardly breathe."

Madis answered him, "I didn't find you. I think someone found both of us – well, all three of us, and brought us here to recover."

Sergey sat up, holding his stomach as if protecting himself from something. He gazed around, whispering, "Palmse."

"Yes, I think so, but how would anyone know? And why bring our host here as well?" Madis pointed to the third person lying on the carpet.

"What is Alexey doing here?" Sergey asked.

Madis shook his head. "None of this makes any sense. Who knew that both of us wanted to be here? Home for you and me, but hardly for Alexey."

Sergey glanced about. "This used to be the music room. Yes, there is my piano."

"Your piano? You said your father used to manage a farm in Lahemaa. I wondered at the time, if you might have meant Palmse."

"Yes. I hated it here then. No friends. Expectations I didn't want. Guilt."

Madis was about to ask Sergey about the guilt when a lovely young lady walked in.

"Ah, Sergey. I thought you might never wake up."

"Anja?" Sergey stood to greet her. "Could this be willful, exasperating Anja?"

She laughed, "The same. Why don't you introduce me to your friend?"

Madis studied her slight face and dark hair – a sprite with very dark eyes. "I am Madis Ak," he said. "Can you tell me how we got to be here all the way from Narva?"

"Is this not where you wanted to be? We understood . . ."

Madis glanced about "Not exactly in the manor, but close to here."

"Oh, yes," she said, "But how is it that you wear the new Eesti uniform?" She fingered his insignias. "Colonel? They tell me you were conscripted by the Russians when the Soviets took your father and grandfather. Were they afraid you might be a religious if they merely left you here?"

Madis rocked back on his heels. She was blunt and even hurtful. He did not ever want to talk about those times – the time in the mountains of another country, missing his father and grandfather while fighting for a government he hated with all his being.

Sergey said, "Anja, do not poke at another just because you are angry with your lot."

She laughed, and Madis recognized the laughter – a voice he had heard at the Narva – a voice that had sung beautiful poems written by a local poet.

"What about your lot has angered you?" Madis asked. And then he realized he was probably trying to hurt her as she had hurt him. "I'm sorry. Perhaps it is . . ."

She turned away and strode down the hall.

Madis spoke to Sergey. "I didn't mean to . . ."

"Oh yes, you did," Sergey said. "But she will have to work out her own wounds. Do you know how we arrived here?" He gestured at Alexey the taverner. "All three of us?"

"I don't. I wasn't awake for the journey. Shall we try to wake him up?"

"I suppose, but first, I want to know something. I was very sick on the drive back to Lake Peipsi. So, I've no idea how anyone found me."

Madis sat down on the nearest worn chair. "That is odd. I became very sick after you left. The last I remember was falling into the bathroom at the tavern and landing on the legs of someone who lay on the tiles there."

They both looked at Alexey. Sergey whispered, "You don't suppose . . ."

"The person may have been him. He had gone to the back before I became sick."

"Those men. They came just as he delivered our dinner."

Madis nodded. "Our dinner and his beer."

"They surrounded us . . ."

"Poison in our drinks."

Sergey nodded. "Rescued and transported home? How?"

Alexey moaned. "Turn it off," he shouted. "Turn the damned thing off."

"What's he talking about?" Madis asked.

Sergey sat heavily on the floor next to Alexey. "Didn't you hear it when you woke up? The cymbals, the drum . . ."

Madis stared at him. "The clinking tune that was out of tune?"

"Yes, can he be hearing it as he awakens?"

"But it is not on." Sergey looked about the large and drab room. "I don't see anything here that might make that awful noise. It was taken to the basement years ago."

Sergey stood and wandered the room and out into the hall before coming back. "I remember that noise – not the music, but the cymbal and drum. There used to be a music box – a huge piece of ugly furniture, but my mother had it taken to the basement after . . ."

Suddenly others began coming toward the room, a crowd of men and women in various forms of dress.

"It has happened, at last," one woman said to another. "We can celebrate tonight."

"But we must dress the ballroom," the other said.

"And unearth our finest."

Their host, Alexey, sat up next to them. "What is happening? This is not The Hermann."

Sergey put his hand on Alexey's shoulder. "We are not sure. We seem to have been very sick and were brought here to recuperate."

Alexey glanced about him and Madis knew he was seeing the drabness of the room.

Alexey said, "Where is here? Why here? Why not home?"

One of the men came toward them, a man of about fifty years of age, dressed in a brown, rumpled Russian-made suit and creaking new shoes. He said, "Madis Ak, you are officially now the manager of Palmse Manner."

Madis stood, "But . . . manager? How can I be manager?"

"You must be. The newest arrival of the correct lineage."

Sergey rushed toward the man. "Father! Then it was all a mistake. You did not die."

The man hugged Sergey. "All will be made clear, soon enough, son. I am very happy to have you with us."

"Father, how do you know Madis?"

"Oh, over time, we all know each other. There is to be a ball tonight because of the happenings in the world – we haven't had a ball any of the time that I have been here – not since 1941, so all the inhabitants are very excited."

"A ball? Mother will be very happy, I suppose."

"Oh no, son. She was forced to leave because of recent events."

Madis could see that Sergey was puzzled.

Sergey asked, "What recent events?"

"The pulling back of the tanks. The Estonians are free. We celebrate the change of regimes. We celebrate the end of an era."

Sergey was truly out of his depth, but Madis could understand. Yet, he hardly believed what he heard, and he knew the upset must be a grave blow for Sergey.

Why did it not seem to be a blow to Sergey's father. Had he not been the manager here at Palmse? And why would the man be so happy to announce that Madis now had become the manager? Madis had never wanted such a job. He had no skills for such a job.

By now, there were about a hundred people in the ballroom. They clearly were planning the evening with great delight and a cacophony of chatter.

Alexey stood beside Madis, complaining. "What the hell is going on? Why am I not in Narva with my wife and children? Who brought me here?"

Madis put an arm around Alexey's shoulder. "Well, it seems we Estonians have something to celebrate. When this evening is all over, let's take you home. Perhaps, as manager of the place, I will be able to find a truck or a car to drive you back to Narva to join the celebrations there."

Though Russian, Sergey seemed as delighted by the change of regime as any Estonian might have been. He joined the others in planning the entertainment. Among the crowd that arrived were several musicians.

As soon as the salon was decorated, with old curtains swiped to one side with satin bows, and all of the worn chairs pushed against the walls, the musicians urged all to retire to their rooms to change to ball attire.

Madis pulled Sergey aside. "I´ve never owned anything that might even pretend to be a suit for an event like this."

"Nor have I, any longer, such a suit. Let us retain our uniforms."

"Yes," Madis nodded and brushed his suit coat. "This is probably the best we might have."

Alexey suddenly took an interest in running the party as only a great host might do. He said, "There must be a wine cellar in such a house," and he left the room on the hunt.

Many minutes passed, with Madis taking more interest in assisting with the décor, even going to the garden to bring in a few branches of evergreens to fill two vases that sat on the mantel piece.

Alexey returned. It appeared he had raided the basement for liquor and wines.

He commandeered a table to set up a bar and ordered some of the crowd to help him by serving. His new recruits set up tables that he found in various rooms of the old manor and had chairs put around them, leaving a large space for the dancers.

Sergey joined the musicians, playing the piano.

When all the members of the household reappeared, Madis grew very curious. He couldn't believe that on such short notice they could find fabrics and ballgowns from so far back in the history of the area.

Some wore ancient Estonian dress – billowy skirts of all stripes, embroidered blouses and hats. Some wore gowns from the eighteenth century, tucks, flounces, skirts held up by hoops of varying crazy shapes, high collars, low hemlines and sleeves wide at the top but suddenly narrow at the wrist. Hair piled high and bosoms plumped low. Every century in between appeared on the dance floor.

During the re-entrance of the fashion show, Madis wandered into adjoining rooms. At the back of the stairs, leading to the second floor, he found a door that seemed hidden.

He opened it and saw that it led into a basement. He remembered Sergey saying something about his mother and the basement. Alexey had brought all the liquor for the party up from the basement. The switch nearby turned on one dim electric bulb.

Madis noticed that this electric addition to the old manor was done with a wire running from a hole in the wall, probably bringing electricity from the main floor to this location. The wire ran across the right-hand wall and down to the bulb above the bottom stair.

Madis walked down the stairs and hunted for another switch for the rest of the basement lights.

What he found was an old flashlight. He hefted it, and found the switch quite shiny and worn, as if it had been used over and over again. He used its feeble light to glance around.

Well, he thought, *if I'm to be a manager, for whatever reason, I may as well get a look at the foundations of this place.*

And then, he found the wine room. Many dusty bottles and a few smashed ones, as if someone had thrown them against a wall. Had there been a fight down here? Even the broken pieces were dusty, so a fight or a moment of pique for someone quite a few years ago.

He'd have to ask Alexey what he made of this collection and its apparent lack of care.

In another room, he found a cot and mattress, also covered with dust. He tried to think about the person who, in all the rooms of this house, might have slept here.

And then in yet another room, he came upon a tall and dark wooden cupboard – nearly black wood, possibly mahogany finish, black with age.

He opened the door of that cupboard, and found he was facing an eight-inch drum. Two small mallets hovered over the drum. Off to the right of the drum inside the cupboard sat a small copper plate that seemed to be convex. Madis plinked his fingernail against the copper and was not surprised to discover this was the cymbal sound he had heard as he woke up on the lounge carpet.

Below the drum he saw a small set of piano-like strings of perhaps two octaves. Piano-like hammers hovered over the strings.

A little lower, he found plectra which would have enacted the hammers and the drum and cymbal. However, at the bottom of the music box, an empty space sat, where there should have been a cylinder with protrusions to move the plectra. Off to the right, a geared mechanism waited for the impulse to run the music box, but as Madis studied the whole outside of the music box, he could not find a way to supply an impulse. He thought he remembered the first woman's voice telling someone to stop cranking, but there was no crank.

A flattened piece of metal seemed to encompass some wire or other form of power, and it reached from the gears to the outside on the right, but it attached to nothing.

And now Madis realized the geared mechanism could not work even if it had an impulse of power. There were gear sizes missing such that one gear could not mesh with another to push anything forward.

The whole thing seemed like a squirrel cage merry-go-round without a squirrel. There appeared to be no way to turn the mechanism on.

So Madis had no idea why he, and evidently also Alexey and Sergey had heard this machine playing as they woke up. Madis wondered if there could be two such machines in one manor house. An unlikely purchase, he thought, since whatever he had heard had not sounded at all pleasant.

The door to the basement opened. He heard footsteps on the stairs, so Madis returned to the bottom of the stairs.

Stepping lightly down to the basement, he discovered the first dark-haired woman who had earlier mentioned the fate of his father and grandfather. He noticed that she had not dressed in any period costume for the event of the evening. She wore a cotton dress that he remembered her wearing earlier in the day. However, this time he noticed that a red stain marred the dress just below her sash. The sash had covered it more thoroughly this morning.

"Anja?" he said, unsure if he remembered her name properly.

She stopped two stairs above him, which put her on his level — face to face.

"Yes, I am Anja." She stared back into the darkness. "I once used this as a place to hide. It was good until my mother discovered the wine cellar."

"You hid from your mother?"

Anja turned toward him. "I must tell you that my comment about your father was meant in solidarity. My father also was taken away. He objected to having his farm collectivized. Plus, he was Jewish. Gone since I was four years old, and I still miss him."

"I'm sorry," Madis said. "I see how you meant the comment. Did they want to take you, also, because you and your mother might be Jewish?"

"My mother betrayed him. I did not know it at that time, of course, but I learned later, from my father."

"Your father has returned from Siberia?"

"He is upstairs, in the ballroom. Come up and meet him."

Madis stared at her. He understood from the revelers that, somehow, they had won freedom from the Soviets, and the celebration was because of that change of regime, but how could her father already be here? Did a change of regime bring home all who had been dragged so far away?

If so, might his own father . . .

"I will come up, but please answer two questions for me?"

"Yes?" she said.

"Might my father also be upstairs already?"

"I believe it is your grandfather."

"What? How can that be?"

"I don't understand yet, myself," she said. "But your second question?"

"This machine down here. Is there another like it upstairs somewhere?"

"Never. There was only ever one and it only made noise if you bumped it." Anja suddenly put her hands to her head. "He bumped it. That is all he did."

Madis didn't understand what appeared to be Anja's anguish, but he realized he didn't understand most things since he came here. And now he was going to find his grandfather, but not, evidently, his father. Had not Grandfather died after all?

As he followed Anja upstairs, he realized that she was really quite beautiful. The amazing truth was that he had not thought about that fact since the first moment she had come into the room.

Not thought about something that once consumed his energies, and, if he let it, his dreams.

At the top of the stairs, he tried putting his hands on her waist, just to test his reaction, but she seemed to slip away, leaving his hands empty. And, in truth, he didn't mind that fact.

Not my type, he guessed. *No vibes.*

Upstairs, the music had started. Men and women danced together – an old dance for couples that he had seen in movies – a reel, he thought, or a line dance, or . . . he had no idea.

As Anja crossed the room, Sergey stood from the piano. He said something to Anja and let her slip onto the bench. She began playing old songs that Madis recognized – Estonian songs that he had heard at the song fests and at the Narva River. Most of the dancers listened, but some, those in more modern dress, began singing along with her. After a few verses, the men and women in earlier costumes sang with the others, as if they were hearing and learning these songs for the first time.

They liked the sentiment, learned the words and tune quickly and were delighted to know the songs. What surprised Madis was that they had not heard them many times before. These songs were his country's resistance – sung in defiance of the Russians at every song fest and then at impromptu events – sung as they blocked the roads from Russia to other Soviet countries.

As the singing went on, he was able to look over the crowd for his grandfather – or would the man she'd met really be his father who might still be alive?

He could not find him.

A woman dressed in a silk gown with a hoop skirt came to him. "Why are you not singing?"

"I am . . . I like listening."

"They tell me you were at the Narva River with others, singing."

"I was at the Narva, until I became very sick."

"Oh yes," she said. "So, they tell me. And you were the first Estonian to return from that effort. Congratulations on becoming the new manager here at Palmse."

He shook his head. "I have no idea why I should be the manager here. I live in Illumagi."

"Yes," she said, fiddling with a fan that she drew from the voluminous folds of her dress. "Illumagi, so close, and Estonian, so you automatically become the new manager."

"That makes no sense," Madis said. "I know only farming and, thanks to the Soviets, I don't know much about that."

"Do not worry," she said. "All will be well. Ah, the young lady is playing a waltz. Let us dance."

Madis had no idea how to waltz, but he felt it would be rude not to dance with a friendly person, so he put his hands out and let her guide him.

After he had tripped on her gown twice and then finally learned where to put his feet, she laughed and said, "We older ones should teach you youngsters the old ways."

He glanced at her fine skin and bright eyes. "Older?" he said, "Are you being a bit modest?"

"It is too bad we only have this evening. This chance only comes once in a great while."

"And I'm thinking that if I am called on to manage here, I will be far too busy to learn any dances, new or old."

"Oh, do not worry. There is always a Hands-on Manager at Palmse. Some have been better than others, but they will be taking care of the real work."

Madis thought a moment. "Do you mean there will be a handy man who does whatever is needed?"

"Certainly. A hands-on manager who survived the events at the Narva and returns to care for the manor. I understand he is on his way, bringing the body of our musician." She pointed toward Anja at the piano.

"I'm sorry to hear that. A musician died at the Narva."

"Of course, her soul flew home, but he is caring for her body, so they say."

Madis tried to make sense of this statement, but the woman bowed to him as the waltz ended. He realized that he had never felt the texture of her dress and had no idea about the shape of her waist, though they had danced for at least three minutes.

She floated away to greet someone dressed more like herself, so he moved toward the bar and Alexey.

"Mine host," Madis said. "Is this not the craziest party you have been able to serve?"

"It is, Madis Ak. I am finding that none of this wine has much flavor, but it seems to be keeping the guests happy."

"What do you make of the rumor that the tanks have pulled back and left Estonia to its own devices?"

"I have heard it from many. They seem to believe it."

"It is impossible," Madis said.

"It is impossible that you and Serge and I are all here – far from the Narva and so fast."

Madis stared about him. Something about this party, about this crowd and its ballgowns, about the fact of the music box . . .

"Alexey, when you woke up, you shouted for them to turn something off. What were you hearing?"

Alexey gazed off at the windows and the evening light. "I think it was a drum, some tinny sort of cymbal and a piano up in the highest keys – very tuneless, like the piano strings had not been tuned for years."

Madis nodded. "That is what I heard as well. But that mechanism is in the basement and cannot operate."

"You mean? Wait," Alexey said, "that ugly cupboard next to the wine cellar?

"Yes. Drum, Cymbal, piano strings and hammers, but no gears and no way to operate the plectra."

"How can that be? There must be some way. We both heard it."

"I think Sergey heard it as well."

"There must be a recording of it, then. That's what we heard."

Madis laughed. "Ah yes. Why didn't I think of that?"

"But," Alexey said, glancing around to be sure no one heard him. "It was so awful. Who would record that shit for posterity?"

Madis nodded. "And then bring it out for a party?"

Alexey said, "This fellow Jergen that she told to stop cranking it – that fellow must be a little bit noodle headed."

Madis smiled. "You are so right, brother."

Sergey came to talk to them. He looked perplexed, and a little afraid.

Madis asked, "What's going on, Sergey?"

"Something doesn't make sense here. They say Soviet tanks pulled back yesterday, but yesterday, you and I and Alexey were in Narva. We would have heard that if it were true."

"Is the radio tower broadcasting?" Madis asked.

"Good idea. If they are sending out the usual tripe, we will know it is not true. If it is not sending, we will know the tower is being contested."

Alexey said, "That monster tower? The Soviets will never give that up."

"I'm afraid I agree," Sergey said. "Let's find a radio."

The three of them left the ballroom and the giddy dancing guests. In the kitchen, they found a radio, They also found a mess – a dinner half created and abandoned – a dinner for four people, not for the mob that presently filled the ballroom. The radio was on, and announcing the freedom of Estonians. The back door had been left wide open, and on the back porch they found an apron, left as if it had been ripped off by someone who ran out of the manor.

Here it was night. No one had eaten this dinner, and the cook clearly was not in the building.

Sergey turned to the others. "The cook here has been a dedicated woman. Her son was a friend of mine, Estonian. His mother would not have left the kitchen for any but the greatest emergency."

"Or," said Madis, "Perhaps for the greatest celebration. Where is her son now?"

Sergey shook his head. "I believe he would be wherever Anja is. He loves her more than anything. But he is not here, so, I don't understand."

"Anja, who took your place at the piano?"

"Yes," Sergey said. "The other weird thing is that her father has returned from Siberia. How can that be when the Soviets merely pulled back yesterday."

Madis shook his head. "And she said that my grandfather is here, but I am certain my grandfather died in Siberia, in my father's arms."

"All right," Alexey said. "We have to go back in there and find this grandfather of yours and learn how he came to be here, and why?"

"Sergey," Madis said. "They tell me I'm to be the manager here, but what about your father? And what do they mean there will be a hands-on manager?"

"My father died," Sergey said. "He is here. But he supposedly died while I was in Afghanistan. My mother must have lied about that. She took over as manager by sheer force of will and nastiness."

Madis hesitated, and then he asked, "You hate your mother?"

"Vehemently. She beat anyone who got in her way."

"And that included you?"

Sergey nodded and then glanced toward the piano. "And she beat Anja and my Estonian friend. I would not be surprised to discover that she beat my father, given an opportunity."

Madis frowned. "Maybe that explains something I heard before you awoke. A woman said that your mother was being forced to leave. When someone asked if she were going to take you, another answered that you left instructions that she was not to have you."

"Not to have me?" Sergey asked. "But those were instructions I gave to my commanding officer and sent a copy to the cook – my friend's mother. Those were instructions about my body, in case I died."

"In case you died," Alexey said.

Madis thought this situation made no sense. Why would anyone here know of Sergey's instructions? Of course, the cook Sergey had known was nowhere to ask that question.

Furthermore, he, Madis, certainly was not going to stick around as a manager, especially if there was no real job. He needed to go back to school or on to a viable job if the stand-off with the Russians truly was over.

And that rumor about the tanks pulling back – he had a hard time believing. He didn't trust any news coming out of Moscow, or out of the nearby tower, or even from the Narva.

He would keep his uniform and his side arm at the ready and see what craziness happened.

He looked about for his father or his grandfather – another thing he could not believe until he had proof. Why would Anja know his grandfather might be here? He didn't even know Anja.

Madis watched her playing the piano. Sergey had been correct to give her the keyboard. She played as if she loved to play. Sergey played well, but as if he were forced to do it.

After a few songs, an older gentleman leaned over Anja's shoulder and said something to her. She smiled at him, lifted her hand toward his. He laid his hand on her shoulder, and she caressed his fingers there.

Then she began to play a song Madis recognized from an accordion and a clarinet duo who played in the square in Tallin. A klezmer band . . . a special song for . . . for whom?

Another man stood behind the man who had asked her to play this piece. The second man was stooped and bearded, but the eyes – Madis knew those eyes. He walked as if in a trance toward the man.

"Vanaisa? Grandfather?"

The man straightened. "Oh no," he whispered. "Not little Madis, too. . ."

"Yes. Madis. Grandfather how did you get here?"

The old man hesitated a moment, but then put a hand on Madis chest. "Do you feel that?"

Madis looked down. "I see your hand there."

"What do you feel?"

"Yes, of course, I feel very happy. Very happy to see you, but how . . .?"

"How did I arrive here?"

"Yes. It is so quick. The tanks pull back and the next day . . ."

"No, my pojapoeg. I have been here a long time, resting and becoming re-oriented to the new rules."

"New rules?"

Grandfather said, "Take your wrist in your fingers."

Madis did as he was told.

"Do you feel your fingers there?"

Madis looked at his fingers. "No, but they are there."

"And your pulse?"

Madis glanced up again at his grandfather. "No."

Grandfather replaced his hand over Madis' chest. "No beating?"

"No."

Grandfather shrugged – a small gesture of fatalism. "My beloved. We have this night to celebrate together. I want to hug you to me, but you won't feel it. I want to explain everything, and then we will sleep again until . . . I hope we will not be reawakened, because that would mean another change of regime in our battered land."

Madis feared he understood. He looked about him at Anja and the red stain below her sash, at the women in their dresses from three hundred, two hundred, fifty years back in the history of his country. He glanced at the window, where the gray light of dawn began to shine over the cottonwood trees. He felt a great urgency to know all.

"Grandfather, where is father?"

"Still alive in Siberia, that place of misery."

"Oh, father . . ."

"I miss him as well," Grandfather whispered. "I love you, my honored grandson, but I wish . . .."

"Grandfather, at least we know that others are free. The Eesti, all the Baltic peoples."

"Yes, this night, for them we can feel great joy."

Notes About These Last Stories

Most of the stories in this anthology are pure fiction, some with an element of fantasy and others a nod at the fantastic storytelling of my ancestors – tall tales designed to keep kids around the fireplace when they might otherwise have 'gone snipe hunting'.

The stories 'How to Build a Wooden Boat', 'The Palmse Music Box' and 'The Other Side of the Palmse Music Box' are also fiction. They are an attempt by the author to recreate the fear and joy that took place in those days in August 1991. A choir from Tallinn visited our choir in Portland during the days just after the tanks pulled back from the road to Riga and from the borders of the Baltic Countries.

Among our Estonian friends, jubilation and stories abounded, and also worry about what they would find when they returned. Two years later, our choir visited theirs in Tallinn in 1993. We all marched together to the Lauluvaljak – the outdoor theater.

They were kind enough to have put a band in front of our choir that played a march by John Phillip Sousa. Such a warm and welcoming time, and again, the jubilation at celebrating the whole festival in their own language with their own stories and poems.

The characters in this story are all created by the author. I have only one photo I took of the Palmse Music Box when we visited there. It was blackened by age with few hints of what it once may have been. It wasn't in working order. The internet and other sources are not at all helpful about the mechanism, so I have based this description on what I know of other, decidedly lesser, music boxes.

The event at the television/radio tower did occur and was central to the final recognition by the Soviets that pulling out was their best option. As Imre says, "No man wants the world to see his tank run over children." Velo Rand, a friend from Arsis, our Estonian choir, was a radio music director and announcer, and was at the tower when a human chain and the courage of two Estonian police and all the radio announcers kept the Soviets from taking over that main source of communication.

About the songs in the music box

Below are the original German words of Die Moorsoldaten, The Bog Soldiers. This song, originally written in German prison camps, became a world-wide symbol of resistance, translated into many languages and used during the Spanish Civil War and later. Pete Seeger recorded an English version of the song in 1972.

Here is the original version of the song in German.

Die Moorsoldaten

Wohin auch das Auge blicket.
Moor und Heide nur ringsum.
Vogelsang uns nicht erquicket
Eichen stehen kahl und krumm.

Wir sind die Moorsoldaten
und ziehen mit den Spaten ins Moor.
Wir sind die Moorsoldaten
und ziehen mit den Spaten ins Moor.

Far and wide as the eye can wander,
Heath and bog are everywhere.
Not a bird sings out to cheer us.
Oaks are standing gaunt and bare.

We are the peat bog soldiers,
Marching with our spades
to the moor .
We are the peat bog soldiers,
Marching with our spades
to the moor.

Words by Johann Esser and Wolfgang Langhoff
Music by Rudi Goegel, adapted later by Hans Eisler and Ernst Busch

The bog camps were originally for Socialists and Communists and others who were enemies of the Nazi party, but, of course, their use expanded drastically later.

Composer and writers of the other songs mentioned here:

This is My Song, tune Finlandia by Jean Sibelius. Words for the English hymn are by Lloyd Stone vs. 1 and 2.

O, The Steppes, by Nikolay Sokolov can be heard sung by many choirs.

There is a Birch Tree in the Field (or See The Little Birch in The Meadow) is a Russian folk song. The tune will be familiar to fans of Pyotr Illyich Tschaikovsky.

Kalinka-Malinka, by Ivan Larionov was sung in the play he wrote in the mid-1800s, called Vasilyev Evening. By now, it is often considered a folk song.

Eesti Lipp, composer Enn Vörk, words by Martin Lipp

Mu Isamaa On Minu Arm, poetry by Lydia Koidula and music by Gustav Ernesaks. Lydia Koidula is so revered in Estonia that her likeness appeared on Estonian money up until the Euro went into use. Gustav Ernesak's bigger than life statue is at the top of the hill that overlooks the Lauluvaljak outdoor song theater, the theater where he conducted many choirs during his lifetime.

All of Anja Saarela's writings are by me. Her fierce independence inspired the words.

Facts About the Battle at Ball's Bluff

Information found at Civil War Sites Advisory's Commission (CWSAC)

http://npshistory.com/publications/battlefield/cwsac/report.pdf

The Battle at Ball's Bluff, also called Harrison's Landing, Leesburg

Location:	Loudoun County
Campaign:	McClellan's Operations in Northern Virginia (October-December 1861)
Date(s):	October 21, 1861
Principal Commanders:	Brig. Gen. Charles P. Stone and Col. Edward Baker [United States]; Brig. Gen. Nathan G. Evans [Confederate States]
Forces Engaged:	3,600 total (US 2,000; CS 1,600)
Estimated Casualties:	1,070 total (US 921; CS 149)
Description:	Confederate Brig. Gen. Nathan "Shanks" Evans stopped a badly coordinated attempt by Union forces under Brig. Gen. Charles P. Stone to cross the Potomac at Harrison's Island and capture Leesburg. A timely Confederate counterattack drove the Federals over the bluff and into the river. More than 700 Federals were captured. Col. Edward D. Baker (a U.S. Senator from Oregon and a friend of President Lincoln) was killed. This Union rout had severe political ramifications in Washington and led to the establishment of the Congressional Joint Committee on the Conduct of the War.
Result(s):	Confederate victory
CWSAC Reference #:	VA006
Preservation Priority:	III.2 (Class B)

Acknowledgements

A deep gratitude can be felt by the world for the work of the Baltic countries of Lithuania, Latvia and Estonia. Their "Singing Revolution" proved to all that persistent, non-violent confrontation can work miracles. From 1987 to 1991 they persisted.

In frequently blocking major roads and the border while singing and refusing to back down, they attracted the world's attention to their work for freedom. Yes, many lost their lives to this effort, and many lost their livelihoods. But they persisted and they sang.

They taught the rest of us that "No man wants the world to watch his tank run over another man." Their courage and the world's consistent attention to their effort freed them from Soviet rule.

In 1991, the Portland Symphonic Choir had made a visit to Estonia when it was under Soviet rule. This was during the "Singing Revolution" described in the Palmse stories. They were welcomed to Estonia by Arsis, a large choir from Tallinn.

I want to thank members and families of the Arsis Choir and Handbell Choir of Tallinn, Estonia for their friendship and their music. It was from the members of this choir that we learned of the history of their struggle for freedom, the loss of fathers, grandfathers and brothers to the Soviet fear of opposition. Many Estonians there knew that their family members were taken to Siberia but had little or no word about their lives after their disappearance.

The first choir visit to Estonia happened right at the end of the "Singing Revolution". Afterward, they came to visit us in Portland just as the tanks were pulled back and the Baltic countries (Estonia, Latvia and Lithuania) were freed.

Our visit to them again two years later happened as they were beginning to realize that they could now enjoy starting their own businesses, live a life free from the fear of disappearance and celebrate their own stories, music, literature and art.

They had a new and elected government. Their world now began to reflect their own culture. As shown in the stories here, they were learning that not all Russians who still lived in their country were part of the oppressor – that Russians had also been the oppressed. How to live together was a frequent topic of discussion.

The denominations on their fiscal bills (Kroons) were only one demonstration of their celebration of Baltic freedom. The faces on the bills were their leaders who supported the work toward freedom in earlier times and during the Singing Revolution. One bill celebrated their national poetess, Lydia Koidula. This was the one country I have visited where the money did not only depict historic politicians.

These bills were eventually superseded by the euro. That European alliance is now a great part of their strength in the face of new Russian aggression on past Soviet satellites such as Ukraine.

*   *

In our youth, we had a friend I will call Ilya who had come from Latvia, another of the singing Baltic countries. His family had escaped from Soviet rule because his uncle had already been taken to Siberia by the Russian government and they were certain his father would be next. He once described to me their fear as the ship they were aboard evaded torpedoes when they sailed into the Baltic Sea.

As with many in the Baltic countries, Ilya sang. As an adult, Ilya also was a member of the Portland Symphonic Choir.

A year after the Baltic Countries earned their freedom, Ilya came to visit my husband and me. He wanted to tell us he was about to take his mother's and father's ashes back to their newly freed homeland because that was where they had always prayed to be buried. Sadly, Ilya himself died not long after his trip to Latvia.

* *

In the remaining stories in *The Palmse Music Box*, I wanted to celebrate other miracles made possible by members of my family and friends. Though I have changed their names, they have recognized themselves in the stories and know that I appreciate our shared experiences. They and I hope you will enjoy these small wonders as well.

About the Author

Rae Richen is the author of adventures for adults and young adults, of romantic suspense and of the forthcoming number two in the *Glyn Jones and Grandma Willie Mystery* series. Join Rae Richen as we explore fear and power, greed and human need in short stories and novels, articles, interviews and essays.

Using family relationships and the backdrop of historical events, Rae Richen writes to bring focus to the themes that drive our human race. The characters in these stories face a confusing world of hypocrisy with courageous honesty. The humor, friendships, and caring they bring to these situations help them forge new solutions to age-old problems.

Learn more about this author at www.raerichen.com or contact her at rae@raerichen.com .

How This Anthology Came To Be

The stories in The Palmse Music Box were written over a period of years. When it came time to look back at the stories I had produced, I realized that several of them, those I have put into this anthology, have dealt with small miracles.

I foresee other anthologies coming your way because as I wrote the nine novels you presently are reading, I took time to relax by writing about events I saw happening around me.

Watching and participating in life triggers questions: Why would anyone do that? What might have happened if that person had reacted more (or less) violently? How could the people in that situation have prevented the disaster that just happened? What causes some folks to buy into a blatant load of lies? Why are some people afraid of many things?

Each short story attempts to find answers to one or more of these questions. So, while I work on the next novel, I hope you also will join me as I explore such conundrums in shorter stories.

I'll keep you updated on what is coming your way when you join my guest area at www.raerichen.com/guest-area. While you are there, you can read first chapters of my novels.

Enjoy!

Also by Rae Richen

For a good read of all first chapters, and the history and back story of these novels, sign in as the author's friendly reader at https://www.raerichen.com/guest-area .

Uncharted Territory – a father-son adventure in the mountains and in learning to accept and love despite the fragility of life. Learn more: https://www.raerichen.com/books

Scapegoat: The Price of Freedom – Gib Evans, a teen, and his friends struggle with a culture of easy accusation during the McCarthy Anti-Communist era. They work to save their favorite teacher from accusations of treason. Learn more: https://www.raerichen.com/books

Scapegoat: The Hounded – after September 11, 2001, a grandfather and grandson work to create safety and freedom for friends falsely accused of treason. The grandfather is Gib Evans, depicted in *The Price of Freedom*. He and his grandson, Alexander, face a new era of easy accusation and the use of fear to control others for the sake of power. Learn more: https://www.raerichen.com/books

In Concert – A novel of suspense and romance when a famous musician is stalked by a vicious man who wants to own her and her son and her extremely valuable manuscripts. Visit https://www.raerichen.com/in-concert and read the first chapter for free.

Frozen Trust – a novel of espionage and romance within the United States during World War II. Visit https://www.raerichen.com/frozen-trust and read the first chapter for free.

Sentinels of Solitude – a novel of suspense and love during a murderous land grab in the lush Willamette Valley of Oregon. Visit www.raerichen.com/blog for the stories behind the story.

A Fool's Gold – a novel of treachery and romance in the Rocky Mountains of Colorado during the mining fever of the 1880s. Visit www.raerichen.com/books for more information

Those Who Curse You – A Murder Mystery of Unlikely Bonds and Unrelenting Peril – Can inner-city architect, Sarah Rohann and her client, Abraham Hallowell save their families from the murderous drug gang that threatens all of their lives?
www.raerichen.com/books

Without Trace: A Glyn Jones and Grandma Willie Mystery – When Trace Gowan, drummer in Glyn Jones' hip-hop band, goes missing, Glyn and his friends involve Grandma Willie and her connections to prison and police in the search. They find there is a lot more than a kidnapping going on and all of them are in danger.
www.raerichen.com/books

Coming Soon: *Calling The Shots, An Anthology of Short Stories:* A confection especially for readers who asked "What happened to Elizabeth in The *Price of Freedom?* To Dick Street of *In Concert* and in *Those Who Curse You?*"

Learn what caused Gryf and his brother Sam to be the targets of a madman even before they came to the United States – the back story of *A Fool's Gold.*

And see what happened to Lewis James's missing brother, Dicken – a follow-up on Lewis's search for Dicken during *In Concert.*

In this and other anthologies soon to be published, Rae Richen has given us short stories to reveal where these characters lives intersected with the stories in the novels and where they went after we last saw them.

At the same time, in other tales, Rae Richen tells us stories of whole new worlds and characters that you will want to follow and cheer for as they attempt to untangle their complicated lives.

www.ingramcontent.com/pod-product-compliance
Lightning Source LLC
Chambersburg PA
CBHW050616190726
48283CB00007B/2443